BE THOU
MY VISION

Hymns of the West #2

BE THOU MY VISION

Faith Blum

First Edition
October 2014

ISBN-13: 978-1500890537
ISBN-10: 1500890537

Cover design and interior formatting by Perry Elisabeth Design (http://perryelisabethdesign.blogspot.com)

Church image © sumners | canstockphoto.com
Folded paper image courtesy of ba9160 | sxc.hu

Be Thou My Vision is a work of fiction. Names, places, characters, and incidents are from the author's imagination. Any similarities to real people, living or dead, are entirely coincidental.

All Scriptures are quoted from the King James Bible as found on www.biblegateway.com.

For Naomi who was always so patient
when I would talk about people (characters)
she didn't know while we did the dishes.
Thanks, Sis!

CONTENTS

A NOTE FROM
THE AUTHOR

One of my beta-readers noted a couple of times that she didn't know some of the words I used. Instead of getting rid of the Scottish/Irish words and accent, I decided to add a glossary. All the Scottish words I used, and their American equivalents, are listed below.

Glossary of Scottish Words

Bairn............	Baby
Da.................	Dad, Papa, etc.
Dinna...........	Did not/Didn't
Ken...............	Can
Kenna..........	Cannot/Can't

The proverbs of Solomon the son of David,
king of Israel;
To know wisdom and instruction;
to perceive the words of understanding;
To receive the instruction of wisdom,
justice, and judgment, and equity;
To give subtlety to the simple,
to the young man knowledge and discretion.
Proverbs 1:1-4

He that getteth wisdom loveth his own soul:
he that keepeth understanding shall find good.
Proverbs 19:8

PROLOGUE

This was taking too long. Aishlinn's pains had
started early the afternoon before and this
afternoon was almost over. Would either of them
survive? Iain stopped his pacing and shook himself.
Of course they would. Aishlinn wouldn't desert
him like this. He resumed his pacing. It seemed like
days since the doctor had kicked him out of the
house earlier that morning. He looked up at the sky,
the sunlight was already starting to wane which
meant Caleb and Anna would be back from school
soon.

Iain's gaze shifted toward the fields behind the
house and he sighed. There was still so much work
to do there. As much as he wished his eleven year
old son, Caleb, could help him in the fields, today
he was glad both Anna and Caleb had been at
school.

"Da?" a small voice next to him spoke up. "Is
the baby here yet?"

So they were home. He hoped the bairn would

hurry so he wouldn't be stuck with too many questions. Iain patted his daughter's unruly red hair. "Nay, Anna. The wee bairn isna here yet."

"When will the baby come?" she asked.

Iain raked his fingers through his hair. "I dinna ken, Anna. I just dinna ken."

"It's been a long time," Caleb said.

"Yes, it has." Iain scowled and continued his pacing.

"Da?" Anna piped up. "How long did it take for Caleb and me to be born?"

"Less time than this one," Iain snapped. "Why dinna ye…"

His sentence was swallowed up by the outraged cry from a small set of lungs. Iain turned to the door and entered. He paused in the front room, unsure where to go. Should he enter the bedroom or not? As he stood frozen in place, the doctor stepped out of the bedroom, his face an emotionless mask as he held the small, wriggling bundle.

He glanced up. "It's a boy." The doctor's voice was flat, his face full of grim foreboding.

Iain looked from doctor to baby, he knew the answer before the question left his mouth. "And Aishlinn? How is she?" His voice cracked.

The doctor finally met Iain's eyes. "There was nothing we could do."

Iain shook his head. It couldn't be. Aishlinn couldn't be dead. Her God would not allow her to leave her husband with three children to raise on his own. Iain brushed past the doctor, abandoning his new son to reach his wife.

As he entered the room, the midwife was

pulling the sheet over Aishlinn's face. He let out a strangled cry. "She kenna be dead," he whispered. The midwife tried to give him a sympathetic look before leaving him alone, but he ignored it. "She kenna be." Iain lifted the sheet off the body. Aishlinn's lifeless face had a contented smile on it. Her eyes were closed and if he hadn't known better, he would have assumed she was asleep.

But as his hand brushed her cheek, the slight chill working its way through her body made him shiver with disgust. Iain closed his eyes, tears threatening to leak out the corners. He collapsed on the chair, holding her cold, stiffening hand.

"Aishlinn. How could ye do this to me? I need ye here with me. I kenna raise three bairns on me own. Ye know that! How could ye leave me?" His head fell to the bed and racking sobs shook his body.

The light was fading when he raised his head. As his eyes adjusted to the dim light, he saw Anna standing in the doorway holding something in a blanket.

"Da?" she asked, her voice quiet and timid. "Have you seen the new bairn? He's a strong, handsome lad." Her face held a mixture of grief and joy.

Iain's throat tightened. Anna had always loved those who were weak, helpless, and alone. Even in the midst of her grief for her mama, she still held onto a joy and hope for the boy who had killed her.

"Nay, I ha'e not and I dinna want to. He'll need a wet nurse..."

"Da, I can feed him with milk from the cow. Please let me do it. For Mama?" Anna's large, brown eyes pleaded with him.

15

Iain closed his eyes and swallowed hard. "Wee bairns need to be fed many times both day and night. I kenna ha'e ye wearing yerself out. With Aishlinn..." his voice broke and he took a deep breath. "With Aishlinn gone, we will need ye to do most of her chores. Feedin' a wee bairn would be too much for ye. Especially wi' your school work."

Anna's head drooped. "I can do it, Da," she whispered, giving the baby a light kiss on his forehead. "I know I can."

"Nay, Lass," Iain said, resolve in his tone. "Ye're but nine years old. Much too young to take this much on ye'reself. It will be hard enough for ye to keep the house clean and food on the table."

"I'll help her, Da," Caleb said as he stepped around the door frame. A determined look glinted in the older boy's eyes. "I'll help Anna with whatever she needs help with so we can keep our brother here with us."

Iain ground his teeth together and scowled at his two half-grown children. "Ye do realize he killed ye're mama, do ye not?"

Anna's head snapped up. "What?" A look of betrayal glimmered behind her tears.

Caleb stared at his father. "Are ye daft, Da? He didna kill Mama. There is no way he killed Mama. You will not pin the blame on him." Caleb's eyes flashed with an anger Iain had never seen in the lad before. His eldest son had somehow avoided inheriting either of his parent's quick tempers.

Iain sighed in resignation and stood up. "Fine, we'll keep the lad for now. But, if either of ye starts failing in school or slacking in any of ye're chores,

I'll find a wet nurse for him."

Anna smiled and put an arm around his waist. "Thank you, Da!"

Iain tensed before he patted Anna on the head.

Caleb nodded, his lips set in a thin line as if trying to figure something out. "What's his name?"

"Aishlinn said if the babe was a boy, she wanted his name to be Jedidiah William Stuart," Iain stated.

Anna smiled down at the bundle in her arms. "Welcome to the Stuart family, Jed."

CHAPTER ONE

I walked home with fear and excitement in my heart. The letter seemed to burn a hole through my pocket. Oh how I wished I could tear it open right now and read what my little brother had to say. It had been almost seven years since his fourteenth birthday—the day he left—and this was the first letter we had received from him since.

For the first time in years, I felt like running all the way home. But even an old maid like me wasn't supposed to run lest I be labeled a "batty old maid". I rolled my eyes at the thought. Of course, I was already considered batty since I didn't go to church and I barely socialized with folks.

"What is wrong with being batty anyway?" I mumbled to myself. Out loud. Good gracious! It was a good thing no one else used this road. The number of times I could have been caught talking to myself would be rather embarrassing.

Taking a quick look around, I saw I was near the fields where Da and Caleb were working. I picked up my pace. "Caleb! Da! We have a letter from Jed!" I waved the letter at them. Caleb looked up from his work with a grin a mile wide. He was like that—almost always happy-go-lucky no matter what happened. I wished I could be that way. Da glanced toward me before getting back to his work. He wasn't one to show much emotion, especially when it came to Jed.

I strode to the house in a rather unladylike fashion—who would see it anyway, much less care? I put away my purchases and had started to look around the living room to figure out what to do next when Caleb and Da clomped into the kitchen. I smiled with satisfaction. Caleb had convinced Da to come in and get the letter reading over with. Good!

As I took the letter out of my apron pocket, I walked through the doorway into the kitchen. Caleb looked at me with anticipation written all over his face. He fiddled with his hands—clenching and unclenching, gripping and ungripping them— like he always did when nervous about something. Da kept his eyes glued to the wall, trying to pretend he didn't care what Jed had to say. I knew better. He did care in his own way, if for no other reason than because he was curious about what Jed had been doing the last seven years.

Caleb was the first to speak. "What's it say, Anna?"

I looked to Da for permission to read. He gave a curt nod and I tore the envelope open. It held two different letters. One was written by a man I did not know and I chose to set it aside in favor of Jed's letter. Jed's familiar handwriting beckoned to me from the paper. His handwriting was still the same as when he was a child, scrawling all over the page. The paper had an almost Jed-like smell to it. I swallowed hard before my emotions got the better of me.

The letter was lengthy by his standards. Even as a boy, he had never been wordy about anything.

The paper crinkled as I unfolded it with care. I took a shaky breath before beginning to read.

> *Dear Da, Caleb, and Anna,*
>
> *It's been awhile. I left afore I was barely old enough to take care of myself. The day I left is ferever imprinted in my memory. Its the day my life changed completely. At first it was for the better. I was away from Da's fists and would never again have to worry about bein' beaten by him. Then I joined up with a gang of outlaws.*
>
> *For the first time, I felt I had become part of a family, one who saw me as more than just someone who existed because his mama died.*
>
> *I'm ramblin'. I'm really not sure how to say all I wanna say. I have only a few more hours left to write and now that I get round to it, I find it harder than I thought it would be. First thing ya need to know is that in a few hours, I will be hanged for rustlin' and horse thievin'. By the time this letter arrives, I'll be dead. Don't lose yourselves in grief for me. I deserve this punishment and worse. I have done lots I shouldn't have.*

The words were choked out by the lump that rose to my throat. As I attempted to regain my composure, I saw Da glaring at me. I closed my eyes and took a deep breath. The lump subsided enough for me to continue reading.

What you need to know most is that because of three forgivin' people who were bold enough to ignore my insults and surliness, I won't be in a livin' death for eternity. When I die, I know that I'll go to heaven.

Before I get into that, I need to apologize. Da, if yer still alive, I'm sorry I beat you up. At the time, I thought it the best way to stop you from doin' that to me. I thought it'd make me feel better and it did for a few hours. I wish there were a way to go back in time and change what I did. I should've found another way to stop you. If I had, there'd be a lot of people still alive who deserved life more than I did.

Caleb, when I left, I didn't think of what it would do to you. I'm sorry if because of my leavin', you got stuck with lots more work. You always tried to be there for me. Thank you.

Anna. Dear, sweet Anna. I thank God for Anna who was a rock in my life. She was the one I knew I could always count on. I know my leavin' must've caused you plenty of worry and heartbreak. You always were, and will be, like a mother to me. I really hope yer married and have a passel of kids by now. You'd be a wonderful mother. I know you were to me. I'm sorry to have caused you any worry. And now I know you'll be grievin' for me, too. Do not let it overpower you like Da did with Mama. I'm in a better place.

I suppose it's now time to get back to what I was talkin' 'bout before my apologies. I'm a Christian. I can't believe how wonderful I feel now. It's like the weight of a hunnert anvils came off my shoulders and I can finally walk free. Jesus truly does save. He is the only One who can.

As I write, my mind keeps goin' back to the song

22

you often sang to me, Anna. "Be Thou My Vision". I don't remember the Irish and wouldn't be able to write it out anyhow, but I remember some of the words in English. "Be Thou my vision, O Lord of my heart; Naught be all else to me, save that Thou art, Thou my best thought, by day or by night, waking or sleeping, Thy presence my light."

My voice broke at the remembrance of these words and my vision blurred as the tears came to my eyes. I took a few shaky breaths and refused to look at Da.

That is what I want for all three of you. May God truly be your Vision, your Light, your Life. God's Word tells you how.

I was the worst of sinners. I murdered many, many times. I did despicable things to people to satisfy myself. I cussed like the best of 'em. I hated you, Da. I hated that Caleb never tried to step in to stop you. I hated that all Anna could do was cry over my wounds and do her best to soothe and heal them. I was ungrateful and selfish. I deserved death.

God wanted somethin' different. He wanted me to be a follower of Him. By the time I listened to Him it was too late for me tell others about Jesus Christ. If I could've done somethin' different, it would've been to learn of Christ's love sooner and share it with others. I know I won't have much, if any, impact on people. But if I can do one thing before I die, it'll be to tell you about Christ. I pray it helps some.

We went to church some as kids. I remember Caleb, Anna, and me walkin' to church many times. I remember some of the things the preacher said. None of what I am going to say should be too new for you.

Here are the basics as Sheriff Brookings and Miss Harris told them to me. Because of Adam and Eve, we're all sinners and always will be. Because of sin, we should all go to hell. Look at Romans 3:23 and 6:23. Then God did something incredible. He sent His Son to die for everybody's sins. Miss Harris said that if there had been only one person on earth, Jesus would've died on the cross so He could save that one person from eternal life in hell.

Because of Jesus' sacrifice, we now have a way to get to heaven. All we have to do is accept it. It's free, but not easy. It requires surrenderin' our lives to His will. Acceptin His gift means we become His servants. The good news is that He is a kind, loving, and forgiving Lord.

Da, Caleb, and Anna. Please think about this. I want to see all three of you again someday. In a few hours, that won't be possible on this earth. I am prayin for you. If it is allowed, I will be prayin' for you in heaven, too.

Your lovin' son and brother,
Jed William Stuart

As I read his last salutation, "Your loving son and brother," I broke down completely.

Caleb stepped forward and wrapped his arms around me in a gentle hug.

"Shh. It's okay, Anna. He's in a better place now."

"But he's gone. My baby brother is gone," I sobbed.

Caleb held me at arm's length. "He chose his path."

My sobs slowed down as I took a few deep breaths. "I know. It's just…I was practically his mother." I put a hand to my chest. "It feels like a knife was thrust through my heart." Two more tears trailed down my cheeks.

Caleb nodded. "I know. I always thought he'd live longer than I would because of all he went through as a kid. He was tougher'n all of us."

I glanced over to where Da stood motionless against the kitchen table. "Da?"

His head rose slowly. "Jed's gone. Fittin' somehow that he'd a-been hung." Da swallowed once and slapped his hat against his thigh. "After what he done ta me b'fore he left, he oughta been hung." Da looked past me toward the door. "Well, Caleb, time's a-wastin'. Let's get back to work." He walked out of the kitchen door.

Caleb and I stared after him. I knew my eyes must have looked as big as saucers. My jaw felt like it was about to fall to the floor. Caleb shrugged his shoulders and followed Da out the door.

As soon as Caleb left the house, I picked up the envelope from the table, realizing I had forgotten about the second letter. I unfolded it and looked at the signature. Joshua Brookings. Wasn't the sheriff's name Brookings? I looked at Jed's letter again. Yes, I was right.

I started to read the short letter from Sheriff Brookings. One paragraph in, and I decided to wait until later this evening. Maybe I could get my emotionless lug of a brother to read it to me. From what I had seen, Sheriff Brookings wrote about the details of Jed's death. With the state my emotions were in right now, I would never be able to read it on my own.

I spent the rest of my afternoon alternately cleaning and weeping, and sometimes both at the

25

same time. I still couldn't believe Jed had died. Every day of the past seven years, I had clung to the slight hope we would hear from him, but I had always known he was alive. At least, I had assumed he was. Now? Now, I knew without a doubt he was dead.

My emotions were all over the place. On one hand, I was ecstatic that we had finally heard from him. On the other...well, he was dead and we would never see him again. I paused at that thought. What had Jed said? That we could see him again in eternity? I walked with a reluctant, yet eager, gait back into the kitchen and took Jed's letter off the table. I re-read the last part of his letter. Yes, I was right. He had said that we could see him again.

As I read his explanation a second time, my heart grew heavier and heavier which didn't make sense to me. I'd considered getting saved once, but Da had forbidden it and that was that; I hadn't thought of it again. So why now? Why after all these years of suppressing those thoughts would they have to come back again?

I didn't think I would ever be able to do what Jed said I would need to do. Da would kick me out if I ever did something like that. Not to mention I would have to give complete control of my life over to someone whom I couldn't see. I shook my head with conviction. No way. God obviously didn't care much about me anyway.

Back when I was younger, I had always dreamed of getting married and having lots of kids. Yet here I was; an almost thirty year old spinster who had never had anyone remotely interested in courting her. If God had cared about me, wouldn't He have given me a little hope of my dream coming true? If not that, couldn't He have made Jed write me at least one other time while he'd been gone?

I took a deep breath and shook my head with unnecessary violence. I had to get my thoughts off of all this. I looked outside to see where the sun was hanging. Almost time to start supper. No sense in putting it off. I trudged through the yard to the cellar door, pulled it open, and clomped down the stairs. I filled the bucket with potatoes, carrots, and a jar of canned venison, topping the bucket off with a jar of apples.

Back inside, I cut up the vegetables and put them in a stew pot with the meat and some water and set the pot on the stove to simmer. Then I worked on the apple pie.

As I rolled out the crust, my mind wandered to the first time Jed had tried to help me make pie crust. He had been determined to help me as much as a four year old could. He took everything out that I needed and started dumping the ingredients together. Every time he had seen me make it, I had measured the ingredients with a pinch of this, a handful of that, and a spoonful of the other thing. I guess he decided he could do the same thing. The crust ended up a bit sweet, but otherwise, it was salvageable. I just made sure I didn't add any sugar to the filling.

Tears threatened to pour out of my eyes again. "Stop it!" I scolded myself. "Just stop it!"

The pie had finished baking when boots

27

stomped on the steps outside. After adding a piece of wood to the stove, I took a quick glance around the kitchen. The stew was hot, the biscuits were ready, the table was set, and the pie was on the back of the stove staying warm. The only things missing were my sanity and inane cheerfulness. I closed my eyes for a few seconds and took a shaky breath. I doubted I would ever regain that cheerfulness. It had all been a façade, anyway. Now I didn't need to fake it.

Caleb and Da walked in as I reopened my eyes. Caleb's grin told me two things. Number one, he hadn't been as affected by Jed's death as I had—either that or he hid it better than I did. And two, they had finished harvesting one of the fields. I made a weak attempt at a smile. "Supper's ready."

"Good! I'm starved." Caleb walked around the table and collapsed into a chair.

I controlled the urge to roll my eyes at the typical response from Caleb and instead, dished up the stew. Once the three of us were seated, Caleb and Da dug into their stew and biscuits with abandon while I picked at my food. After they were finished, I served the pie. As I handed them each a plate, I mentioned the second letter.

"Caleb, would you read it? Please?" I pleaded. "I tried and couldn't. From what I could tell it was from the sheriff and he told about how Jed died." I may have been a spinster and almost thirty years old, but that did not mean I wasn't susceptible to the normal womanly emotions. At least, I hoped they were normal.

"Sure. Where is it?" I envied Caleb's emotional detachment. Was I the only one affected by Jed's death? Or were they affected in a different

28

way? I wish I knew, but none of us really talked about...well, anything really, but especially not our emotions.

I dug the letter out of my apron pocket and handed it to Caleb.

Dear Stuart Family,

It is with heavy heart I write to inform you of the death of your brother and son. Jed asked that I write you more details on the why and how of his death. He was an outlaw and had been for seven years. His crimes for the first five years would not have put him in jail because there was not enough proof of his involvement.

Two years ago, he robbed a stagecoach. In the ensuing shootout, the driver and shotgun guard were killed leaving the two passengers as the only survivors. The two survivors were me and my younger sister. By God's grace, we escaped. Jed was the only member not killed or wounded and he came after us, but we were able to elude him. After he realized he would not find us, he went on a wild rampage. In his anger, he violated a young lady.

I gasped, unable to stop myself. Caleb glanced over at me and cleared his throat, then continued.

Throughout the next two years, he tried to find Ruth and me while he did odd jobs here and there. Sometimes he hired out as a gunman. For the last year, Jed had been rustling. His abilities as a gunman were not "needed" as often, and he needed money. In the end, that was how he got caught.

Jed and his two partners tried to rustle cattle off the wrong ranch and we were waiting for them. It was the rustling that got him hung.

Jed was in my jail for nearly two weeks. During that time, I did my best to convince him that God cared for him and would forgive him of all his sins. He wouldn't listen to me. I telegraphed the young lady, knowing she had not pressed charges even though she did know his name. I prayed she was a Christian and would be willing to help convince Jed that God could indeed forgive him.

It took a couple of days, but God broke through his stubbornness using the young lady and me.

Jed accepted God's gift freely. It was humbling to see the instant change in him. He went from a sullen, angry, bitter, resentful man to being humble, considerate, and ready to die for his crimes.

Two days after his acceptance of the gospel, Jed was hung. He died as he requested—to the sound of singing. He asked me, my sister, and Elizabeth to sing a particular song while he was hung. The song was one my family and I taught him the night before, "A Mighty Fortress is Our God". It was hard to keep the tune going because of our sorrow at our new friend's death. Even now as I write, the sorrow hinders my words. I've never seen any man more composed and sure of himself than Jed was that morning. I am proud to have called him my friend.

Enclosed you will find Jed's death certificate. If you have any questions, please feel free to write. I would be happy to answer any questions you may have.

Sincerely,
Joshua Brookings
Sheriff of Cartersville, Montana

CHAPTER TWO

By the time Caleb finished reading the letter, I was crying silently. Caleb's voice had also become subdued by the end of the letter. I couldn't believe Jed had done all those things.

"He really is dead," Caleb whispered, his voice husky with emotion. "How could he have done those things? My little brother. He was always the one who stood up for what was right."

"He got involved with the wrong crowd," Da snapped. "Of course he did those things. Why shouldn't he? He ran off afore he was old enough to care for himself. The outlaws turned his mind to th' wrong things." Da stood up and stretched his arms above his head. "I'll go check on th' stock and then get off to bed."

"Da, I can check the…" Caleb started.

"Nay, Lad, I'll check th' stock. No reason for you to do it. I'm not that old a man yet." Da strode out the back door without a second glance.

My crying slowed and I was just getting the tears to stop when Caleb spoke again. "What'd you think about this God talk?"

I closed my eyes and took a deep breath. It was a very good question. Ever since I had read Jed's letter, thoughts about God had not been far from my mind. "I'm not sure yet. I think I might start reading the Bible more to see what's so special about it." I lifted my eyes to Caleb's. "What do you think?"

"Mama believed all of it. She was always reading that Bible of hers and talking to us about it." Caleb got a faraway look in his eyes. "She loved that old book." His eyes came back to focus on me. "Da won't like you reading it, Anna."

I lowered my head. "I know." I swallowed hard. "I'm also considering going to church."

Caleb's eyes widened. "Da would like that even less and you know it. He'll never let you go!"

"He doesn't need to know I'm going," I said. "I have nearly a week to figure out how to sneak out to church. I'll think of something." I stood up and worked on clearing the table. "As for reading the Bible, I can do that while you two are out in the fields and in the evenings when Da goes to bed." I leaned against the sink, facing Caleb and crossing my arms. "It's high time someone in this family became more sociable with the people around here. When was the last time we did anything sociable?"

Caleb stared at me with a blank look on his face. "The barn raising... Three years ago?" he answered after a long pause.

"Four years ago. And as I recall, you and Da said next to nothing while I kept myself busy with doing as much as possible so I wouldn't have to talk to anybody."

Caleb screwed his face up in concentration. "I suppose we have been like hermits lately."

"Ever since Jed left," I interrupted. "Even though he was the most shy of us all, when he left, we got more and more unsociable. Now, I hardly know who anybody is in town. I couldn't tell you what happened to my best friend from school."

Caleb shook his head. "How did we let this happen to us? It's no wonder neither of us is married and has ten kids. No one knows we exist."

"At least you would still be able to marry. You have land you will inherit, not to mention you are pretty good looking, even if you are nearing middle age. Me on the other hand? I'm a plain-looking spinster who talks too much, speaks her mind too freely, and can keep a house clean and food on the table. No, you, Caleb, are our only hope to keep the Stuart line going."

I turned around and started washing the dishes. Determination filled my voice after another moment's thought. "Yes, that will be one of my goals when I start going to church: To find you a wife."

Caleb sputtered. "W-what? Are you daft?"

I laughed. For the first time in years, I let out an honest-to-goodness laugh, one that doubled me over and seemed to shake the windows. Then I realized the shaking windows had been Da slamming the door shut.

I looked toward Da and saw him glaring at us. "So, I'm out there checkin' on th' stock while ye two are in here caterwauling about who kens what?"

Even Da's incessant bad mood couldn't wipe the grin off my face. "I was only teasing Caleb about finding him a wife, Da. Don't you agree it is high time he find himself a wife?"

Da stared at me as if I had sprouted horns and my unruly red hair had suddenly turned to raven black and straight as a level board. He shook his head and stalked up the stairs to his room. I bit my cheeks to keep the smile and laugh from bursting forth yet again. Da would likely fly into a rage if I dared to laugh at him.

Instead, I chose to glare at Caleb, although the glare effect was probably lost behind the broad grin still on my face. "Nay, I am na' daft." I purposely chose to let my Scottish accent come through, knowing how much Caleb disliked it. "I'm as sane as ye are, Caleb."

Caleb rolled his eyes. "Sure y'are."

My mood left without warning. "Caleb, I either laugh or I cry. I choose to laugh. If I don't…" My voice trailed off as I could no longer speak without crying.

Caleb nodded. "I suppose that's true. You're taking this harder than any of us."

I grabbed Caleb's arms. My voice was tight and low as I spoke. "Caleb, who raised Jed? I did. I raised him almost single-handedly. Da did nothing to turn him into a man worthy of the Stuart name. Da kept you too busy outside for you to help me raise him. I'm the one who raised Jed from a wee bairn to a man."

I let go of Caleb, suddenly deflated of all energy. My voice dropped to a whisper, "When Jed left, I knew he wasn't ready to face the real world.

34

Old enough, yes. Wise enough?" I shook my head. "I kept hoping, and yes, praying, he would come back. When he didn't..." a sob crept through my words. "You know what I did. I retreated from life. I stayed away from everybody."

"I know," Caleb said, his voice quiet. "We all did."

I took a deep breath and looked outside. "We need to get to bed."

Caleb nodded and stepped forward to help me.

We were both silent the rest of the night. Caleb put the dishes away while I dried them. Then we each made our way upstairs to our rooms.

I fell asleep immediately, my heart and all my energy completely spent.

After picking at my eggs and biscuits the next morning, I tried to go about my normal chores. By mid-morning, I was drained both in soul and body. I had tried not thinking about Jed and what had happened to him. When that didn't work, I tried thinking about Jed. Neither one worked and all I did was drain myself of what little strength I had left and dissolved into tears.

I somehow managed to get lunch on the table through my crying and serve the meal while suppressing the tears. It must have tasted decent, too, since Caleb and Da shoveled it into their mouths. After Caleb and Da returned to the fields, I decided to go to town. Maybe being around strangers would help.

On my way out the door, a slight ray of light

caught my eye. On a normal day, it wouldn't have caught my attention, except that the light was surrounded in shadow. The ray should never have appeared in that spot. I took a closer look at the shelf where it had appeared. The light rested on Mama's Bible.

"Mama," I whispered. "Jed." I let my fingertips brush the spine and looked up at the ceiling. "God, if you're out there, I…" my voice faded. "God, I can't do this. I can't live like this anymore. Help me. Please."

I lifted the Bible off the shelf and stared at it for a few minutes before backing up toward a chair and falling into it. I opened the Bible up to the bookmark. Mama always kept it in the place she was reading.

"What was it you were reading last, Mama?" I took a deep breath in an attempt to calm my nerves. "What were God's last words to you before you died?"

I began to read at the bookmark. Two hours later, I was engrossed in my reading of the book of John when a faint knock sounded on the door. I put the bookmark back into the Bible, closed it, and set it on the chair.

I hurried across the room and opened the door to find a young woman looking back at me. I stared into her bright green eyes that seemed to bring out the red tint to her auburn hair.

"Hello," she said, sticking her hand out. "I am Wilma Gardner. I recently moved onto the neighboring farm with my husband. I heard there was a woman living here and thought we could possibly become friends. The ladies in town said not to pin my hopes up, but when have I ever listened to people like them?"

In spite of myself, I found my lips curving up into a slight smile. First, this stranger was Southern. Second, this vivacious young woman might be my answer to getting me out of my...whatever it was I was in.

"Anna Stuart," I replied, returning her handshake and inviting her in. After seeing if she wanted something to drink, I continued, "I live here with my brother and father. They're out in the fields."

"Maybe we could have you three over for dinner sometime this week," Wilma offered. "I'm sure my husband would be glad for some advice from men who have farmed here for awhile."

I shook my head. "I doubt that would be possible. Da doesn't like visiting with people and he certainly does not like discussing farming with anybody, not even Caleb."

Mrs. Gardner's face fell. "Oh. Darius will be sorry to hear that." She looked down at her lap. "Perhaps you and Caleb could come visit us?" She glanced up at me, hope shining in her eyes.

"I wish I could give you a more satisfactory reply, but I'm afraid that will be impossible."

"Too bad. Well, we'll just have to be content with what we can get." She smiled, her green eyes lighting up. "Do you go to church?"

I started. "Why do you ask?"

She nodded toward the chair where the Bible still lay. "You have a Bible over there."

"Oh. That." I cleared my throat. "Today was the first time I've read it in...a long time." I shifted in my chair, wringing my hands. "I...I haven't been to church…for almost fifteen years." I looked up. "I am considering going again, though."

I was shocked to see Mrs. Gardner's eyes light up. What had I said to inspire that sudden joy?

"You are more than welcome to join us in our wagon on Sunday, if you don't want to walk or ride on your own."

I forced a smile. "Thank you."

"Is there more than one church around here?"

I blinked my eyes a few times. "No, I believe there is only one."

"Who is the pastor?"

I opened my mouth to answer before realizing I had absolutely no idea how to answer. "I don't know. As I said, it has been almost fifteen years and I know the pastor who was there before is no longer there."

Mrs. Gardner nodded. "You're not comfortable with me, are you?"

I swallowed, nervous about such a direct question. "More your questions than you. Although, I haven't had many friends for awhile. I may just be out of practice."

Wilma laughed. "Well, it is time to change that. Let's start by getting to know each other. May I call you by your first name?"

"Yes, that would be fine. Okay," I said, the word stretching out because I was unsure how to start. "Well…How about you start, Wilma?"

"Yes, ma'am," Wilma said with a wink. "Let's see." She leaned back in her chair and stared at a spot behind me. "Well. I am twenty-three. I have been married for three years to a very wonderful man. His name is Darius, but I think I already mentioned that. We have no children yet, but pray for some soon, Lord willing. I enjoy crocheting, knitting, cooking, and sewing. Pretty much anything I can do inside." Wilma gave me a half smile as she leaned forward and looked me straight in the eyes.

"I have two sisters and three brothers back home in Southern Tennessee," she continued. "I'm the oldest. My parents are both still alive and are very anxious to have grandchildren. I think those are most of the basics about me." She raised her eyebrows. "Now it is your turn."

I couldn't believe how nervous I was. All she wanted was for me to tell her a little about myself. Why should I get nervous about that? "Um," I licked my lips. "I am twenty-nine and have never been married. My mama died when I was nine and I raised my baby brother for fourteen years. I do not like cooking, cleaning, or sewing. I tolerate them because it is necessary for me to do them. I would much rather be outside washing clothes than be inside washing dishes."

I closed my eyes, trying to give no thought to who was in the room with me. "It has always been my dream to get married and have at least five boys. No girls. I wouldn't know what to do with a girl. I know the games boys like, how to get them to do things they never would have done otherwise." My smile faded and my eyes were blurry when I opened them. I closed my eyes again to hide the tears that threatened.

I heard and felt Wilma come over and kneel beside me. "What is it, Anna?"

I took a deep breath. "Nothing," I said. "It's nothing." I straightened and pasted on an almost sincere smile. "Do you have a favorite color?"

"Purple," Wilma said with a smile. "You?"

"Brown."

Wilma moved back to her chair and leaned an elbow on her leg. "Favorite animal?"

"Dogs."

"Cats," Wilma laughed and my smile grew more sincere. I was beginning to like this young woman. Maybe she would let me be a surrogate aunt to her children.

"How many children do you want to have?" I asked.

"As many as God allows, but at least two. Darius grew up as an only child and said he didn't wish that fate on anyone else, if at all possible."

I looked away from Wilma's animated face, unable to bear the sight of her eager expression. "Some would have preferred to be only children," I said. When I saw her confused expression, I held up a hand for her silence. "No, not me. I didn't mind. At least…not until yesterday." I broke off. I hadn't planned on telling her that. I shook my head vigorously, almost throwing the bun in my hair out of place. "But, I do know some people who would have preferred to be the only child."

"But, why?" Wilma asked. "Why would anyone want to be an only child?"

"To have their parents' love all to themselves without having to share it. To not have the competition of besting their older brothers and sisters. To be able to retreat without fear of interruption. I don't know. All I know is that the young man I speak of wished he had been the only child born to his family." My voice dropped to a whisper. "Or that he had never been born at all."

40

Wilma's eyes went wide with shock. "Who is this young man? Where is he?"

"Dead," I said in a flat, emotionless voice. "He was hanged over a month ago." I stood up. "Are you sure you don't want tea, coffee, or water?"

Wilma forced a smile. "No. No, thank you. I'm fine. I should probably be going anyway. It is almost time to start supper."

"I hope I didn't chase you away with my bad mood," I apologized.

Wilma's real smile returned. "Not at all. I like you, Anna Stuart, and I plan to become a very good friend to you." She stood directly in front of me and put her hands on my shoulders, looking up into my face. She was over a head shorter than me, but I had gotten used to that. Even some men had to look up at me. Yet another reason I was still a spinster.

Wilma gave my shoulders a quick squeeze and turned to leave.

"Come again soon," I invited.

She turned her head toward me. "Thank you, I'm sure I will."

With that, she was gone. I looked up at the clock. Sure enough, it was high time to get supper started. I hurried over to the chair, picked up the Bible and put it back on the shelf before rushing into the kitchen. "Well, Da, supper'll be a few minutes late. I hope you won't get too angry about that."

CHAPTER THREE

Saturday night arrived all too quickly for me. I had to make up my mind and make it up fast. Was I going to defy my father and go to church or not? As I heated the water for our weekly baths, I debated back and forth with myself.

"Da would be livid if you went," one side said.

"But, it might help you get some answers to the questions you've had all week," the other side countered.

"*Possibly.* Only *possibly.* You might end up with more questions than answers."

"Not if God truly wants me to get answers."

"How do you know God isn't a fairy tale?"

I sighed at my inner antagonist. "I know Jed. He never lied to me. He might've lied to others, but not to me. Jed said God is real and I believe him."

"Jed turned bad after he left you. You have no idea if he might lie to you now. He probably ended up as a skillful cheat and liar."

My good side desperately wanted to reach out and shake my other side. "Jed would never lie to me. He would also want me to do what was right, no matter the cost." My antagonist tried to rear up and speak again, but my other side hushed it. "No, I have made up my mind. I am going to church."

I bobbed my head down and then back up with deliberation. My decision was made. While I waited for Caleb to finish bathing, I ironed my best dress for the morning.

"Anna, I am finished," Caleb said as he walked into the room.

"Thank you Caleb," I said. I took a deep breath and let it out slowly. "And so you know, I am going to church in the morning. I will do my best to be home for lunch, but don't expect to be. I have fried chicken and vegetables in the icebox. All you need to do is get them out and put plates and forks on the table. Is that all right with you?"

Caleb leaned against the door frame, his arms crossing over his wide chest. "You're sure you want to do this?"

I put the iron down on the stove, "Caleb, I need answers. The only way to get those answers is to go to church."

"What about that new friend of yours? That neighbor lady?"

"Wilma?" I shook my head. "No, I don't think she could answer some of the questions I've got. I need to hear from the pastor and get them from him."

Caleb nodded. "Yes, I suppose so. I'll do my best to keep Da calm. He won't like it. But I'm sure you already know that." Caleb straightened. "I'd best get some sleep."

"Goodnight, Caleb."

"'Night, Anna."

I sneaked out of the house soon after breakfast and walked to the church. The church was situated on the edge of town closest to us so it didn't take very long to walk there. When I arrived, I walked into the churchyard and stopped on the edge. I watched as smaller children played, doing their best not to get their Sunday clothes dirty. There were pockets of adults talking. I suddenly felt out of place, but then, what else could I expect? I *was* out of place. I hadn't talked with people in town or been to church for almost fifteen years.

I took a deep breath and walked further into the yard. Looking around, I didn't see anybody I really knew. Wilma was surrounded by the young wives and mothers and I could tell she loved every minute of it. I looked for someone else who was alone, but saw no one. Seconds after deciding there was no one to talk to, I saw a young lad sitting on a stump all by himself. I crossed the yard to join him.

"May I join you?" I asked.

The boy looked up at me, unshed tears glistening in his dark blue eyes. He nodded and made a little room on the stump. I lowered myself down with care. "I'm Anna Stuart," I said, holding out my hand. "Who are you?"

The boy looked at my hand for a second before cautiously putting his hand in mine and giving it a half-hearted shake. He shook his head.

45

I cocked my head, my eyes narrowing in curiosity. Was the boy mute or shy? "Well, I can't keep calling you 'boy'. Surely you have a name."

A reluctant smile tugged at the corners of his mouth as he nodded his assent.

"Good! Now that we have that settled, I have a question for you: Can you speak?"

His hands moved in a series of quick signs I was unable to understand.

"You are mute?" I guessed. His head bobbed up and down and the shy half-smile came back.

"Well, guessing your name will be all the more challenging now." I put a forefinger on my chin in exaggerated concentration. "Does your name start with a letter between A and M?"

I could almost hear his brain working as he tried to figure out the answer to my question. After less than a minute, he nodded.

"A through F?"

A shake of his head.

My mouth quirked in concentration. "G through J?" I asked.

His eyes lit up and his head nodded with vigor.

I smiled. "Does it start with a G?"

He shook his head.

"H?"

Another shake.

"I? No? Then it must start with a J."

I began to fear the boy's head was going to be shaken off. "Is it a Bible name?" I asked. He nodded his head. "Hm. Jeremiah?"

One strike. "John?" Two strikes. I couldn't remember of another "J" name from the Bible, besides Jed's and I certainly hoped it wasn't that name. I sifted through my limited knowledge of the Bible and finally remembered another one. "James?"

The boy's shy smile grew into a full-fledged grin.

"How old are you, James?"

James held up seven fingers.

"Seven? My, my. You are almost grown up." I was quiet for a minute while I tried to think of a question James could answer.

"Earlier you did something with your hands. Do you speak with your hands?"

James nodded his head.

"He uses sign language," a young voice near me said. I looked up and saw an older version of James standing next to the stump. The older boy gave me his hand. "I'm John. I'm James' brother."

"Anna Stuart," I replied, shaking the offered hand. "Where did you learn sign language?" My eyes flickered between the two boys, taking in their very similar looks. If John hadn't been taller and have an older look about him, I would wonder if the two boys were twins.

John's eyes were the most expressive of the two boys. The pain written in them was heart wrenching.

"Mama taught us afore she died," he said in a quiet voice. "She'd learnt it from a deaf boy when she was growin' up. When we figgered out James couldn't talk, she taught Pa and me sign language at the same time she taught James. Whatever we don't know, we make up."

I looked around the churchyard. Where was the boys' pa? "How hard is it to learn sign language?" I asked.

"Not hard, just time consumin'," John replied.

I tried hard not to wince at the horrible grammar John was using. "Do you go to school, James?"

James nodded, moving his fisted hand up and down with his head. He signed something to me. I cocked an eyebrow at John who interpreted for me with an amused smile.

"He said, 'I can hear, so I can learn everything. The teacher knows not to call on me to answer a question out loud.'"

The church bell rang just then and James jumped off the stump, stood in front of me, and offered me his hand. I gladly accepted it and the three of us walked into church together. Once inside, the two boys walked up to the front row, so I lagged behind and took a seat in the back.

I struggled through the entire service. The hymns were as I remembered them: deep and thought-provoking. The sermon wasn't as I had remembered the sermons to be. Maybe it was because Pastor Jenkins didn't have the same style as Pastor Carlton had when I was attending all those years earlier. Or perhaps it was because I was now grown up and understood it more.

It was hard to sit through the sermon. Pastor Jenkins preached about death. Worse, he preached about the death of a loved one. The passage was from the book of John and was about a man who died, leaving behind his two sisters. Lazarus was one of Jesus' beloved friends. He died and Jesus

48

did nothing to stop his death. Lazarus' sisters begged Jesus to heal him, but Jesus lingered in the city He was in. Four days after Lazarus' death, Jesus arrived and, after some time weeping and grieving with the family and friends, He went out to see the tomb. He ordered for the stone to be rolled away and asked Lazarus to come out.

The main point of the sermon centered on John 11:35, "Jesus wept." The point was that Jesus can commiserate with our pain when we lose a loved one. He then talked about how Jesus and the Holy Spirit can comfort us in our grief.

After the service, I was quite skeptical of the supposed comfort Pastor Jenkins had talked about, but I kept my thoughts to myself. As I had expected, Wilma accosted me nearly as soon as the service was over and introduced me to Darius.

Pastor Jenkins also made sure he welcomed me to the church. He seemed a bit preoccupied and did not talk to me long. I was grateful for that and made a quick escape.

I strode home as quickly as I could without being too unladylike. When I arrived, I sneaked a peek into the window. No one was around. I sighed in relief and let myself into the house. I crept up to my room and collapsed backwards onto my bed, lying there for a few minutes staring at the ceiling. As I lay there, I tried to think of nothing. When I finally allowed my thoughts to return, they went back to...Mama? What was she doing? I held my breath as I allowed myself to be transported to that memory.

* * *

Mama was in the kitchen, sweeping the floor and humming a song. While she hummed, the words ran through my head.

"Be Thou my vision, oh Lord of my heart,
Naught be all else to me, save that Thou art--
Thou my best thought, by day or by night,
Waking or sleeping, Thy presence my light."

* * *

Tears came to my eyes, it had been a long time since I had thought about Mama singing that song. Mama had sung it so often that I knew all the words by heart. Even now, I could still sing it in either Irish Gaelic or English. Tears threatened to spill over my eyelids.

Shaking the thoughts out of my head, I leaped off my bed and hurried into the kitchen. I put together a quick lunch and ate it.

Caleb came in a half hour later. He found me sitting in the living room staring out the window. If he had asked me what was outside the window, I would not have been able to tell him.

"Welcome home, Anna," Caleb said. "How was church?"

I shrugged. I had no idea what to say. Was it good or wasn't it?

Caleb crossed his arms and looked down at me with an arched eyebrow. "What about the sermon?"

"It was...interesting," I said. I knew I was being vague, but I really did not want to talk about it. "If you wanted to know more, you should have come with me." I moved to walk past him, but he caught my arm.

"What's wrong, Anna?"

I glared up into his face. "Nothing. Now let me go!"

He let go of my arm and I left, but not before seeing concern creep into his eyes. What was he concerned about? Me? He didn't have to worry there. I wasn't about to change simply because a sermon hit me in the wrong place or because Jed had died. I stopped in my tracks. The sermon hit me in the wrong place? Was that why I was so out of sorts? I shook my head, trying to get the wayward thoughts out.

The rest of the day I felt like I was hardly able to do anything right and I definitely couldn't do anything fast. Da didn't notice, but Caleb kept a close eye on me all day.

That night, I actually slept well and woke up feeling refreshed and unaffected by my weird sensations from the day before. I breathed a sigh of relief.

The day went well until a knock came at the door. I stared at it for a minute. Another visitor? Wasn't one unexpected visitor a week enough? Then I remembered Wilma had said she would be coming over again. I assumed the visitor must be her and pasted on my best smile as I opened the door. The smile faded when I saw it wasn't Wilma; it was Pastor Jenkins.

CHAPTER FOUR

If I hadn't made a concerted effort to make sure my jaw didn't drop to the floor, it probably would have.

"Good morning, Miss Stuart," Pastor Jenkins greeted me. I unconsciously put my hand into his offered one and we shook hands. My senses came back after the handshake and offered him something to drink. I stepped through the door onto the porch.

"No, thank you. This is a short visit and then I need to be on my way." He settled onto the porch swing. I sat on the rocking chair suddenly glad Da had thought to put it out here for the summer. "I came here to welcome you to our church. I'm afraid I didn't know anybody lived at this house. I have been rather busy or I would have come out to invite you to church when you first moved here."

My eyes widened. "Oh, no, Pastor. You are mistaken. I have actually lived here my entire life. My family attended church for a few years when I was growing up. But then Da forbade us from attending. I decided to visit yesterday after an absence of almost fifteen years."

Pastor Jenkins nodded and the corners of his mouth turned up slightly. "That puts a different light on the situation. Why did you suddenly decide to come back to church?"

My back stiffened. Who did this man think he was to assume I would tell a stranger that personal of an answer. "That is none of your business."

Pastor Jenkins took a deep breath and nodded. "Well, whatever it was, I am glad it brought you back to the fold. If you ever have any questions about anything you read in the Bible, or anything I say in a sermon, please let me know. I am more than happy to answer them." He stood. "I'd best be going now. It was good to talk to you, Miss Stuart." He paused for thought as I stood. "I believe Mrs. Jones mentioned you live with your brother and father. Is there any chance they might attend church with you sometime? Perhaps I should go out and meet with them?"

"Caleb might attend someday," I said, "but Da won't. I don't suggest you go out to meet them unless you want to be threatened and run off the property."

He raised his eyebrows and gave a curt nod.

"I guess I will be on my way. It was a pleasure to meet you, Miss Stuart," Pastor Jenkins said, shaking my hand again.

I watched him walk to his horse. My mind wandered back to the day Jed left and I had stood in this same spot watching the doctor walk to his horse and buggy after giving Caleb and me a grim diagnosis about Da's recovery.

* * *

"I won't lie to the two of you. It'll be a miracle if Iain lives," the doctor said. "He needs rest and the best care he can get. His bandages should be changed at least every two hours and that salve needs to be reapplied each time." He looked at me, concern deep in his eyes. "I don't want you wearing yourself down to keep Iain alive."

All I could do was nod. Jed was gone, Da was near death, and Caleb was as silent as ever. I kept my thoughts to myself, but with Jed gone and little possibility of ever getting him to come back, Da was all I had. I would do everything I could to keep him alive.

* * *

A sob caught in my throat as I came back to the present and realized yet again that I would never see Jed again. Not unless I did what Jed said and got saved. I hurried to open the door, took a deep breath, closed my eyes and nearly slammed the door shut in my hurry to cut off my renegade thoughts.

"High King of heaven, my victory won,
May I reach heaven's joys, O bright
heav'n's Sun!
Heart of my own heart, whatever befall,
Still be my Vision, O Ruler of all."

I sank against the door as the words ran through my mind and the sob that had caught in my throat finally escaped. I don't know how long I sat there sobbing and I really didn't care. When the tears stopped, I swept them away, stood up quickly, and got back to my housework.

I spent the rest of the day working hard and not thinking. I knew that if I started to think, I would imagine too many things, all of which were now forbidden. All of them were impossible to either obtain or understand: God, a husband, Pastor Jenkins, Jed. No, I was needed here at home to cook and clean for my brother and father.

And clean I did. I scrubbed the kitchen from ceiling to floor. I dusted for the first time in months. I beat and aired out our two rugs. I dragged all three mattresses outside and let them air out. When all that was done, I cooked the fanciest meal I had made in years. I roasted a whole chicken I killed, plucked, and prepared myself; fried some potatoes, made buttermilk biscuits and even baked a cake.

When Da and Caleb came in for supper, I could tell the meal got Caleb suspicious. "This meal is great," he said as I stood to clean up. "But why, Anna? It isn't anybody's birthday and I don't recall any other reason we should be celebrating. Or is this supposed to be a funeral meal for Jed?"

I glared at Caleb. "No it isn't," I snapped at him as Da left the house. I clattered the plates together as I gathered them. I could feel Caleb's eyes on me and refused to turn around. I knew what I would see anyway. He had always tried to be the concerned older brother, especially when Da stopped being concerned about me. He also

56

somehow seemed to know what I was thinking, even when I didn't know myself.

This time, he probably thought I was out of sorts because of Jed's letter. For once, he would have been wrong. It was more than just Jed's letter. The eyes seemed to not be on me anymore and as I turned to see an empty kitchen, I realized that Caleb had left. I returned to my thoughts.

Then again, maybe it was all about Jed's letter. It was Jed's letter that had gotten me to go to church which had sent the pastor over to visit with me. His letter had gotten me thinking about God. Not to mention his letter had gotten me thinking about what he'd said in it.

I started washing the dishes, scrubbing them with more force than was necessary, but Caleb was in the barn—probably fixing some of the tack—so at least I was safe from his observations.

"I don't think the finish will come off that plate if you use only a dishrag and your hand," Caleb's voice said right next to me.

I jumped. I had been so absorbed in not thinking I hadn't heard him come in. I put my hand over my heart. "Caleb! You shouldn't sneak up on people like that!"

Caleb grinned. "I'm not really all that sorry. Now will you tell me what's bothering you? I've never seen this kitchen so clean and I've certainly never seen you trying to scrub the finish off of a plate."

I scowled and turned back to the dishes. "No, I won't tell you. It's nothing of consequence."

Caleb threw his hands in the air. "Nothing of consequence? How can you say that? You *never* scrub any room from ceiling to floor. Not to mention I can't begin to remember how long it's been since you beat the rugs. And did I see you airing out the mattresses? It's been even longer since that was done."

Caleb lowered his voice. That usually meant he would soften it, but this time, his voice was hard as steel. "And you most certainly do not cook a big, fancy meal for no reason. You hate being inside for so long and you do not like to cook unless absolutely necessary. Anna Aishlinn Stuart, you cannot tell me this is all 'nothing of consequence' because I know you too well for that."

I stared into the dirty dishwater without knowing what I was seeing as his words whirled around, in, out, and through me. After a couple of minutes of mutual silence, I whispered, "Caleb, please leave me alone. It's nothing I'm willing to talk about right now, and I don't want to talk about it with you. I can't talk about it." I turned to face him, my hands clasped in front of me and my eyes avoiding his. "It's something I need to work out for myself. I'll be fine in a few days." *I hope.*

Caleb tried to catch my eyes before he left, but I refused to let him and I knew all I would see in his was the pain of me rejecting his help. He left after a minute and I finished the dishes in peace. Or rather, quiet. There was no peace left in me. Where peace had been a few days earlier, there was confusion. My peaceful life was gone. My clean, orderly, peaceful life lay in shattered pieces all over. I felt more helpless than James. He was helpless to speak, I was helpless to do... well, to do anything.

When the dishes were finally finished, I trudged up to my bedroom and collapsed onto the bed. I slept fitfully all night. My mind was too exhausted to hold up the walls that had kept my thoughts at bay during the day. My dreams followed my thoughts with careful precision. Too careful. Though I remembered only bits and pieces of them, I knew I didn't like a single one.

The next morning, I tried to read the Bible. I had hoped I could find some answers, but all I received were more questions. I knew, from what Pastor Jenkins had said, that I should ask God, but it felt awkward to talk to Someone I had purposely ignored for so long. Especially when that Someone had lived with me for my whole life without me ever acknowledging His existence until recently.

I was glad when noon came around. I could distract myself with making, eating, and cleaning up lunch. After lunch, I put on my shawl and boots and went outside to walk around the yard. I had started to walk to our small orchard to see how the trees were surviving the mild winter when someone called my name. I looked up and saw Wilma coming down the road toward the house.

"Anna!" she shouted as she ran toward me. "I hoped you'd be home." She was breathless when she arrived at the edge of the orchard. "Do you have time for a visit?"

I forced a smile. "Of course."

"Oh, good! Ever since I saw you at church on Sunday, I have been dying to come out and hear what you think of church. I know you haven't been there for a few years and it must have been quite

59

different."

"Yes, it was. Quite different. Last time I saw it through the rosy eyes of a child. This time…" My voice trailed off and I stared into the distance.

"This time what?" Wilma asked as she took a step closer.

I scowled. I looked away and debated what to say. Should I say what I wanted to or should I soften it? Turning my eyes back to Wilma, I stiffened my entire body and clenched my jaw. "This time I saw it for what it really was. A place for hypocrites to go feel good about themselves, repent of their sins, and do whatever penance necessary so they can go back to their sinful ways the rest of the week and still call themselves church folk."

Wilma's jaw dropped and she stared at me, speechless.

I looked away and sighed. "I'm sorry, that was uncalled for. I've been overwrought, emotional, and snippy the last week. I'm not usually…"

"No, I understand," Wilma interrupted. "I agree, some churches are like that and some church goers are as well. In fact, some of them need to hear that." Wilma laughed which was the last thing I ever expected to hear from her after my outburst. "You are quite right, but you also need to remember that not all church folk are hypocrites."

I gritted my teeth and nodded. "Shall we go inside and get something to drink? I can make some tea."

Wilma smiled. "Tea sounds wonderful, if you don't mind." She followed me into the house. I added some wood to the woodstove and put the peppermint leaves into the teapot on the stove.

60

Wilma watched as I stirred it until it almost reached the boiling point. I poured three cups of peppermint tea and left the third cup on the back of the stove. Wilma was already sitting at the table, so I joined her.

"Well, you obviously didn't really like your visit to church," Wilma began.

"Actually, I did like some parts of it. I met two boys before church. They remind me of my little brother." My voice grew quiet.

Wilma furrowed her eyebrows. "I thought your brother was older than you."

"Caleb is older than me by two years. Jed was younger by nine years."

"Where is Jed now?" Wilma asked.

I looked down into my cup of tea and watched it twirl around. "I suppose—since he claimed to be a Christian—he is in heaven now."

Wilma's eyes widened. "I'm so sorry. When did he die? What happened?"

I took a deep breath and fought the tears welling into my eyes. "We found out last week; he's been dead over a month."

Wilma reached over and patted my arm. "I'm so very sorry. It must be hard to lose your little brother."

"I practically raised him as my own. Mama died giving birth to him, so I had to be Mama and sister to him. He ran away on his fourteenth birthday and we never saw him again. That was nine years ago. He became an outlaw and was hanged over a month ago when his crimes finally caught up with him. Apparently a meddlesome sheriff and some of his family and friends convinced Jed to get saved while he was in jail."

Wilma jerked her hand back. "What do you mean by 'they convinced Jed'? He wouldn't have gotten saved if he hadn't wanted to or felt the need to."

I waved my hand in the air as if dismissing the thought. I refused to think that way. If I did, I would have to admit I needed to do the same thing Jed had done. "Well, you may not want to associate with me. I come from a family of sinners—one of whom was an outlaw—we muddle along without church as best we can. As you can see, I'm not exactly stellar company."

"Jesus associated with tax collectors and sinners. When the Pharisees asked Him about it, He said something like, 'A physician doesn't tend to the well, but to the sick.' You're not getting rid of me that easily, Anna Stuart."

I huffed. "Fine. So long as you know what you are getting yourself into."

"I think I already knew I was in for a friendship that would require some pretty hard work." Wilma's face looked serious. I had to wonder if she really was serious.

I had no idea what to say. What does a person say after she admits to being unfriendly, from a family of sinners, and having an outlaw brother? I decided not to say anything. Instead, I stared into my cup of tea. The drink was getting colder as the minutes ticked by in silence. I swirled the liquid around the cup, watching stray peppermint leaf pieces spin around the opposite direction.

When Wilma's voice broke the silence, I nearly jumped out of my skin. I had almost forgotten she was still there.

"The kitchen looks different from when I was here last. Did you do something to it?"

I blushed. Really and truly blushed. I hadn't blushed in years and now I was blushing from complete embarrassment. How was I supposed to answer that? "Um, yes," I stammered. "I scrubbed the whole kitchen the other day."

Wilma nodded as she looked around her. "Yes, that's what it is. The kitchen almost sparkles. You did a very good job, Anna. I wish I had the gumption to do it. How did you get up the energy? Wasn't it too hot to do it in here with the stove going?"

"I'm used to the heat here. Believe me, it gets much hotter in July." I purposely didn't answer her first question. I should have known she would persist.

"Regardless of that, how did you get up the energy to do it?" She forced a laugh. "Now that I ask it, I must sound like a lazy woman."

I shook my head. "No, you sound like someone who doesn't like to do something that isn't really all that necessary."

Wilma had a mischievous look in her eye as she shook her head. "You, my dear, are avoiding my question." She wagged a finger at me. "What don't you want to tell me?"

"Why do you keep persisting on getting it out of me?"

There was a laugh from the door behind me. I spun my head around to see Caleb standing in the doorway.

"Good luck getting an answer from her, ma'am," Caleb said with another laugh. "She's one of the most stubborn women I've ever seen."

"As if you've seen enough women to know that, Caleb Iain Stuart!"

Caleb rolled his eyes before turning to Wilma. "Since my sister doesn't seem to want to make introductions, I'll just have to be forward. I am Caleb Stuart. Who might you be?"

Wilma took his offered hand and shook it. "Wilma Gardner. My husband and I recently moved to a farm near here. While I was in town about a week ago, I was told Anna lived nearby and decided to try to make friends with her." Wilma hazarded a glance toward me with a wink and a grin. "I think we will be fast friends soon."

Caleb threw his head back and guffawed. "If you can get my icy sister to warm up to you, then you have some sort of magical gift."

I glared at Caleb, but it only made him laugh harder. "Why are you in here at this time of day, Caleb?"

"See what I mean?" Caleb asked Wilma. Turning to me he said, "My dear sister, I am here simply to annoy you and to steal some of the tea you so graciously made for me."

"How is it stealing if I made it for you? And how did you know I had made some?"

"I smelled the leaves being poured into the pan," Caleb said with a straight face.

I shook my head in amazement. "Likely story."

Caleb grinned and picked up the extra cup I had poured. "Is this anybody's?"

I gave him my sweetest fake smile and said, "Yours, of course. I poured it specifically for you. Now take it and get out of here."

Caleb saluted with his right hand, sloshing the hot tea on his hand. "Ouch," he said as he licked the hot liquid off his hand. "Yes, ma'am!"

He took a quick sip and said a hasty farewell to Wilma before leaving us alone.

"Is he always like that?" Wilma asked.

"Pretty much," I said.

"How is he not married yet?"

"We don't get to town much."

"I see. So he doesn't meet many girls."

"And he has little interest in getting married," I said. "Although I don't know why."

"Maybe he hasn't found the right young woman yet?"

"Perhaps."

There was a lull in the conversation as we each tried to come up with something else to say.

"I overheard a few of the busybodies at church talking about Pastor Jenkins."

"You were listening to their gossip?"

Wilma blushed. "No, not really. They were talking about trying to hitch him up to one of the single ladies at church. Talking about Caleb reminded me of it." Wilma shook her head. "I just don't think he will go for their matchmaking schemes. I haven't known Pastor Jenkins very long, but he doesn't seem like the type who would like their scheming."

I stared at the wall behind Wilma. "I think you're right. He seems more the type to wait patiently on God's leading."

Wilma's eyes went wide with astonishment.

"What?" I demanded.

"You've met him, what? Once? How did

you…?"

"I kind of have a sense for people," I shrugged. "I sometimes scare myself at how accurate I am."

Wilma laughed. "Are you always accurate?"

"No."

"Too bad. That could be a very useful skill."

For the first time in days, I smiled. It was a bit hesitant at first, but it slowly stretched out across my face. "Yes, it could."

Wilma glanced up at the clock. "Oh dear! I better get going or I will get supper on late again." She jumped up out of the chair. "Thank you for the tea. It was delicious."

"You're welcome."

She turned to leave, but then turned back and came around the table and astonished me by giving me a hug. "I don't know what's going on with you right now, but I encourage you to read the Bible and pray to God for help in understanding it."

Tears welled into my eyes and I swallowed hard. "Thank you."

Wilma let go of me and walked out of the house. I stood staring at the door for the longest time. When I finally realized what I was doing, I shook my head in confusion. Why in the world am I staring at the door? Then I remembered. The hug. The first real, spontaneous hug I had received since before Mama died and from someone I barely knew, no less.

A tear worked its way down my cheek, resting in the corner of my mouth. I shook my head to get rid of the helpless feeling and went back to the kitchen to get supper ready.

CHAPTER FIVE

The next Saturday night, after Da was in bed, Caleb spoke to me about church for the first time since Monday. "Are you goin' back tomorrow?"

"To church?" I asked, stalling for time.

"Yeah."

I took a deep breath and let it out slowly, keeping my eyes away from Caleb. "I haven't decided yet."

Caleb was quiet for a few minutes. I kept my eyes on my mending and assumed that would be the end of the conversation. Then he said, "I think you should go."

My head snapped up and I furrowed my eyebrows. "What? Why?"

Caleb shrugged. "Even though you were a bit out of sorts, you seemed to be a little more peaceful. And all you can talk about is those two boys. Go back for them if nothin' else."

A smile crept its way onto my face. I turned my eyes back to the shirt I was mending. After stitching up a hole, I said, "You're sure Da won't mind?"

Caleb grinned. "If you're gone before he can object, he can't do anythin' about it."

I chuckled. "True. You're sure you want to deal with him, though?"

Caleb's grin disappeared and he shrugged again. "I don't mind. He knows he can't do much to me."

I nodded. "I'll go."

The next morning, I found myself walking down the road toward town and the little white church. "God," I said, "I don't really know why I'm doing this. Caleb thinks it'll be good for me and I trust his instincts. But last week," I paused my prayer—or talk—as a wagon rattled past me. "Last week, I felt like I'd been hit in the head by a ton of bricks. What's wrong with me? Why can't I act and feel like Wilma seems to?"

No answer came during the rest of the walk to town, but that didn't surprise me. I walked into the churchyard and saw James sitting by himself again. I smiled in anticipation of our lively attempt at conversation.

I kept my eyes in front of me, while also keeping an eye on James. I was almost across the churchyard when a male voice called my name.

"Anna Stuart?" the man sounded incredulous. The way he said it made it sound like it was a miracle I still existed.

"Yes?" I asked, turning to look at him. I stiffened when I saw who it was. Justin Roberts, the biggest bully in school when I was growing up.

"What are you doing here?" Justin asked.

"Going to church," I stated.

"Well, yeah, I know that. Obviously if you are at a church on a Sunday you'll be going to the church, but..." He paused and furrowed his eyebrows. "I thought you didn't go to church."

"I thought the same about you. And I didn't until last week, when I decided to start coming again."

"I'm visiting my parents," Justin explained. "I decided not to fight them today, so here I am." His cocky grin and obvious attitude annoyed me as much as it ever had.

"Good for you," I said. I knew my voice held no conviction, but I didn't really care. "Now, if you'll excuse me, there is a little boy I would like to talk to."

"You always did like the boys, didn't you?"

I gritted my teeth at his implication and walked away to the relative safety of James' tree stump.

"Hi, James, how are you today?"

James shrugged.

"Hi, Miss Stuart!" John said as he joined us. "James was hoping you would be here today. We want to teach you some sign language so you can talk to him better."

I restrained my excitement. "That sounds like a wonderful idea."

The time before church started was hard, but rewarding. By the time we had to go inside, James and I had had a fairly long conversation. After learning so many signs, my mind was distracted during church. At least, until Pastor Jenkins commenced his sermon.

"Please turn in your Bibles to Matthew chapter seven." Pastor Miles Jenkins waited until the rustling of pages quieted down. "We will read verses seven through twelve."

"'Ask, and it shall be given you; seek, and ye shall find; knock, and it shall be opened unto you: For every one that asketh receiveth; and he that seeketh findeth; and to him that knocketh it shall be opened.

"'Or what man is there of you, whom if his son ask bread, will he give him a stone? Or if he ask a fish, will he give him a serpent? If ye then, being evil, know how to give good gifts unto your children, how much more shall your Father which is in heaven give good things to them that ask him? Therefore all things whatsoever ye would that men should do to you, do ye even so to them: for this is the law and the prophets.'

"This passage talks about those who know something about God's kingdom, but still seek out His will for their lives or have yet to come to know Him as their personal Savior. There is a big difference between going to church and knowing Jesus personally. Those who only go to church without a personal knowledge of Jesus Christ will go to hell.

"Are you one of those people who comes to this house of God, but you don't read your Bible or know Jesus as your Lord and Savior? Or perhaps you are one of those who believe that all the good deeds you do will get you to heaven. The Bible is

70

very specific and clear about that very issue.

"In this passage, Jesus explains how to know Him as your personal Savior in a simple, yet difficult, formula. Ask, seek, and knock. Ask God your questions. Seek His answers in the Bible through prayer and asking your pastor or a friend who knows the Lord. And then comes the hardest step: Knocking. Knock on the door and ask God for His free gift of salvation.

"Why is this part so hard? Because we think salvation should be harder than simply knocking and asking. I have heard the question, 'Don't we have to DO something before God will accept us?' many times. Or sometimes it is said this way, 'Isn't there something we can DO to earn God's favor?'

"The Bible answers that question with a resounding 'No'! No, there is nothing you need to, or can do to earn salvation. Ephesians 2:8-9 says, 'For by grace are ye saved through faith; and that not of yourselves: it is the gift of God: Not of works, lest any man should boast.' Faith, not works. I guess we should add that to the list. Ask, Seek, Believe, Have Faith, Knock, Accept. That's all there is to it. Simple? Perhaps. But Belief and Faith do not come easily."

Pastor Jenkins looked toward the back wall; his eyes avoided eye contact for the first time during this sermon. "Although I grew up in a God-fearing home, I had a hard time accepting it for myself and making Jesus my personal Savior. And even after I came to a personal faith in Christ, having faith was often hard. When I knocked and accepted Jesus as Lord of my life, keeping my faith in line with God's Word was, and is, the hardest thing I have ever done. Yes, even harder than

71

watching my wife die. Even harder than accepting that her death would ultimately be for the best somehow."

Pastor Jenkins cleared his throat and wiped the tears out of his eyes. "But that faith is what brought me through all those trials and it will continue to do so in the future. Every day I struggle and every day that I persevere is sweeter than the day before.

"How many of you have faith, but struggle with it? Know this, God is stronger than your trial or temptation and, if you ask, He will help you and guide you through.

"How many of you have yet to believe and put your faith in Him? God is seeking you. Do not hide from Him like the Old Testament prophet, Jonah, did. Jonah was told to warn the Ninevites that they needed to repent or their city would be destroyed. He disobeyed, thinking he could hide from God. God found him and Jonah spent three days and nights in the belly of a big fish. When God let him out of the fish, Jonah completed his mission.

"God seeks you just as you are. He knows you are a sinner condemned to hell. All He cares about is that you come to Him so He can save you from an eternity without Him. God does not want a single person to go to hell.

"Are you hiding from God today? Why are you hiding? Is your faith less than you desire it to be? Trust God and ask Him for help. Seek His face. Believe He can help you. Have faith He will accomplish His work in you. Knock on His door and accept His help and be ready for Him to want you to change."

Pastor Jenkins looked over the sanctuary. For

a fleeting second, I thought he looked me straight in the eye, asking me those questions personally. Then he concluded, "Let us spend a minute or two in silent prayer. After that time, I will close us in prayer."

I bowed my head, thinking that I would go through the motions of pretending to pray. As silence filled the sanctuary, the question, "Are you hiding from God today?" flooded my mind. *God, my heart cried. I am hiding from You. I am hiding by going through the motions of attending church and reading the Bible. I am hiding behind my anger at You for taking Mama and Jed away from me. I believe. I really, truly believe You died for my sins and can save me. Help me have faith to trust in You. I am knocking, Lord. I need you in my life. All I've done is make a mess of it.*

Tears were streaming down my cheeks and I didn't dare look up until I had them under control. When I heard people walking past me, I realized I had missed the closing prayer and altar call. I took a deep breath and wiped my cheeks with my handkerchief. I blinked my eyes rapidly to clear out the rest of the tears and slid out of the pew.

Once outside, I took another deep breath of clean, fresh air before trying to escape the church yard and getting stopped by someone. It didn't happen.

"Hello, Anna," Wilma said. "How did you like the sermon today? Did you have any questions about it?"

"The sermon was very good." I hesitated before going on, "I...I prayed afterwards."

Wilma's eyes went wide. "You did? What did you say?"

"I talked to God. I told Him why I was hiding and asked Him to help me believe and to trust Him." I shrugged, trying to act nonchalant.

Wilma squealed and hugged me close. "I'm so happy for you. That is wonderful! I encourage you to keep reading the Bible, but pray before you do. Prayer makes reading so much more meaningful."

I gave a hesitant smile. I needed to process what my feelings about this were before I talked very much about it. Luckily, I was saved by two energetic boys who ran up to me and grabbed my arms, pulling me away from Wilma.

Wilma laughed. "I see you already made friends with James and John."

I grinned and shook my head. "Yes, I did. I guess I'm supposed to go with them."

James and John dragged me back into the church and we sat in the back pew where the two boys occupied my attention quite thoroughly. My head spun from all the sign language words they were teaching me.

I could read the signs better than I could "say" them, but that was fine since James could hear. I should say I could read the signs as long as he went slowly. But that was the problem. When James got excited--and he got excited easily--he talked much too quickly and I had a hard time keeping up with him.

John let out an exasperated sigh. We had been signing for over half an hour and James was signing something with quick movements. "James, I know ya get excited and it's exciting that another adult is willin' to learn how to communicate with you, but you gotta slow down. She cain't read the signs that fast."

James slumped his shoulders, put his hand in a fist, and put his fist on his left shoulder. From there, he moved it in a downward circle toward his left shoulder. I glanced at James' face and he mouthed the word, "Sorry."

I put my hand on his shoulder. "It's okay, James. I've learned a lot today. Thank you for making my afternoon so enjoyable. Thank you both." I gave John a nod. "I need to get back home now. I'll see you two next Sunday."

I walked home with a bounce in my step. The weight I had carried since hearing of Jed's death was gone. Tears came to my eyes. I would still grieve his loss, but now I knew, really *knew*, what he had been talking about. It was true. I couldn't wait to tell Da and Caleb.

My foot faltered and my breath caught in my throat. Da and Caleb. What would they think of this? I shook my head. I didn't have to wonder what Da would think of it. He would rail and rage against it and forbid me from ever stepping foot in the church again. He would rant and rave about me "being as daft as me mither."

I closed my eyes against the sudden onslaught of emotion and tried to think of Caleb's many possible reactions. Curiosity, dismay, and—dared I hope—acceptance. Perhaps I should try to be an example. Show them the change rather than tell them. Was that cowardly of me or not? I had a sudden wish to have Wilma show up at that moment. I needed her opinion and wisdom.

Perhaps I should go visit her tomorrow. I stopped walking for a few seconds as I pondered the thought. That might not be such a bad idea. As I approached the fence, I made up my mind. I would wait to tell Da and Caleb until after visiting with Wilma.

CHAPTER SIX

"Anna!" Wilma squealed when I showed up on her doorstep the next day. "I wasn't expecting a visit from you today."

I looked down at my feet and then back at her. "I hope it's all right."

She gave my shoulders a squeeze and ushered me into her house. "Of course it's all right! Why wouldn't it be? You are always welcome here."

"Thank you. I was hoping I could ask you a few questions."

"I can't guarantee any answers, but I can try. But first, let me get you something to drink. Water, tea, or coffee?"

"Water will be fine, thank you." I tried to follow her into the kitchen, but she waved me into a seat in the parlor.

"Don't you dare follow me in here. I haven't had a chance to clean it up yet and I won't have you seeing it in this condition."

Smiling, I shook my head as she disappeared through the doorway. Less than a minute later, she returned with two glasses of water and we sat down.

"Now we can talk. What do you want to know?"

I took a sip of water and swirled it in the cup while I gathered the courage to ask my question. "When do you know the best time to tell your family about your decision to follow God?"

Wilma raised an eyebrow. "I suppose that would depend on the family. With mine, I told them right away. From the little you have told me about your family, I would probably wait."

I nodded and took another sip of water. "I think Da would have a very negative reaction. So what do I do? Live the same way as before but know I am His follower?"

Wilma shook her head. "Almost, but not exactly. You won't want to live the same way as before. God has specific works He wants you to do for Him. You may be doing some of your same tasks, but God has something else specific in mind for you to do to glorify Him and further His Kingdom." She looked down at the glass in her hand, then back up at me. "God needs to be Lord and Master of your life."

She got up and paced the room in what seemed like agitation. "Think of it this way: President Hayes and the men in Congress make laws that we have to follow. If we don't, the sheriff will put us in jail or fine us. Most of them are simple rules to follow, and are meant to make our lives better. That's the way God is, too, except that He is more powerful and trustworthy and wants a personal relationship with each of us. If we ask

God what He wants us to do that day and let Him guide us and be Lord and Master, in those pursuits, He will.

"Of course then there is the problem of actually letting God do so. It is much easier said than done. You can say you are letting God be Lord in your life, but then something gets in the way and He isn't anymore. Nothing happens to you instantly when you take control back either. You will still struggle with some of the same vices as before, but you have an extra advocate now."

"So every morning, I should pray and ask God to lead me," I stated.

"And in the middle of the morning, and at noon, and in the afternoon, and in the evening."

I sat still, deep in thought for a minute. "I didn't expect it to be very easy, and I guess it's not." I sighed. "I'll just have to do my best and try to keep God as Master." I paused before forcing a laugh. "Or rather, I'll have to allow God to keep rule over me and live with what He wants me to do."

Wilma's laugh tinkled up to the rafters and she sat down. "Yes, you've got that right. I'll be praying for you."

"Thank you," I said.

Wilma waved her hand. "Not a problem. I need something to do while I clean this mess up. Did you have any other questions?"

"Not right now. And I should be heading out anyway. You have dishes to clean up and I have my own chores to do."

"Thank you for coming, Anna. And remember, you are welcome here anytime."

We stood up and I gave her a quick hug.

"You're welcome. Thank you for answering my questions. I will drop in again, I'm sure."

I escaped her tight embrace and walked back to my house. The chores still seemed like drudgery, even when I was praying. Maybe I should try memorizing some Scripture. I remembered Mama teaching me to memorize. I closed my eyes and thought back to that day so long ago.

* * *

Mama was expecting my little brother or sister. I was extremely excited, but very impatient. There were still four long months left before the baby was to be born. I think Mama was getting rather frustrated with me. That's probably why she wanted me to memorize the book of Proverbs. I could read quite well and I was almost nine by then, so I could do most of the memorizing without her help.

One day, she sat me in the rocking chair, put the Bible on my lap, opened it to Proverbs and told me to start memorizing. I wondered how I was supposed to do that. After staring at the pages for awhile, I looked up. Mama was watching me.

"Is something wrong?" Mama asked.

I fidgeted in the chair. "I'm not sure how to start."

Mama smiled. "I suggest you read the first verse out loud, then repeat it without looking at the page. Do that a couple of times and you should be able to memorize it pretty quickly. Once that one is memorized, go on to the next verse. Try to do three verses today and we can review them together later this afternoon."

I grinned up at her. "Okay."

* * *

As the memory flooded back to me, so did the verses I had memorized that day. "The proverbs of Solomon, son of David, king of Israel; To know wisdom and instruction; To receive the instruction of wisdom, justice, and judgment, and equity; To give subtlety to the simple, to the young man knowledge and discretion."

"God," I prayed, "give me wisdom and instruction. Help me to know You. Help me to know Your will for me."

CHAPTER SEVEN

Time passed slowly for me. The next few months were the hardest months of my life. Dealing with Jed's death, trying to allow God to have complete control of my life, being an example to my brother and father—all of it was hard. My work was monotonous and dreary. I tried to find joy in everything I did, but sometimes it was nearly impossible. When it got too bad, I would stop what I was doing and go visit Wilma.

Wilma was such a good friend. She visited me at least once a week, and I tried to do the same. At church, I almost always ended up talking to her—when I could get away from James and John. James and John were what kept me going to church each week. Except for James; John; Hester, the butcher's wife; and Wilma and her husband, no one else had attempted to reach out to me or talk to me. When I tried to talk to them, they would chat for a little and then make some excuse to go find someone else. James, John, Wilma, and Pastor Jenkins' sermons kept me sane during those first few months as a genuine Christian.

One sunny, cool, early summer Sunday, God took me in a direction I never would have dreamt possible. Pastor Jenkins' sermon hit me right between the eyes. He'd preached about being a living example for others and as he preached about ways to do so, I realized I had been failing in that area. When the service was over, I sat in the pew extra long. Between the sermon and knowing Caleb and Da both resented the time I spent at church, I didn't want to leave the peaceful, quiet sanctuary.

The church was empty when I dragged myself out of the pew and headed out the door. As I opened it, the corner of my eye caught a flicker of movement which I chose to ignore. I walked down the steps and was nearly bowled over by two wild boys. With arms grown strong and quick from manhandling two brothers growing up, I grabbed the two boys before they had a chance to escape me.

Turning their faces toward me so I could see who the offending parties were, I was surprised to see James and John.

"What is going on here?" I demanded. "Why are you two acting like wild, heathen men?"

"We didn't mean no harm, Miss Stuart. Honest, we didn't."

I screwed my eyes shut at John's grammar. "You didn't mean *any* harm. Don't you pay attention at school? I know your mama is dead, but doesn't your da do anything to correct your grammar?" James and John both looked up at me with eyes full of...something. I wasn't sure what it was. Disbelief? But disbelief about what?

Holding firmly to a shoulder of each of the boys, I put on my sternest face and said, "Take me to your da, Boys. I'd like to have a talk with him."

James and John marched in front of me and approached a group of men. I tried to recall which one might be their father, but couldn't think of one who might be married, let alone married and widowed with two young boys.

James shuffled slower the closer we got to the group of men. John tugged on James' arm, pulling him along. As we neared the group, John let go of James' arm in disgust and walked up to the pastor, a glare settling on his brow.

"Pa, Miss Stuart wants ta talk to ya." John aimed his glare at me. I fought a smile. The boy knew he was in trouble and that I wasn't afraid to tell his da about it.

As I took another look at the man John was talking to, I gasped and berated myself for not putting it all together sooner. John and James were motherless. Pastor Jenkins' wife had died. I kicked myself inwardly for not figuring it out earlier.

As I criticized myself, Pastor Jenkins walked over to where I stood with James. John trailed his pa. "Is something the matter?" Pastor Jenkins' quiet voice struck me as oddly fitting under the circumstances.

Putting aside all intimidation due to the fact I was about to scold the pastor, I squared my shoulders and spoke, "As a matter of fact, Pastor Jenkins, there is. These two were running around like ruffians and nearly raced into me as I left the church. As the children of a leading member in this town, they ought to learn, and be taught, to behave better than that. Not to mention the fact that John refuses to speak proper English."

Pastor Jenkins looked at John. "Is this true, John? I know you can speak proper English. Why would you do something else?"

John crossed his arms and glared at his father. Pastor Jenkins sighed and turned around to face James. "James, what do you have to say for yourself?" James signed a few things and then shrugged.

Pastor Jenkins stared at him intently for awhile before turning to me. "He apologizes for running into you, Miss Stuart. He claims it was his fault, but I have my doubts about that." Miles Jenkins looked past me and took a deep breath, letting it out slowly. "I apologize, Miss Stuart. I know I shouldn't make excuses, but in this case I have little choice. My wife died almost two years ago, and since then the church people have kept me so busy I have little time for my boys." He raised a hand when I tried to protest. "Yes, I know, I ought to say no to more people. Or get help with the boys. I have tried both, but everybody has urgent things to talk to the pastor about and nobody will take care of the boys. Believe me, I have tried."

While he was talking, I watched his face. He looked exhausted and completely open and honest about what he had told me. He truly was a busy man who tried to keep his church going, keep his church people taken care of, and be both mother and father to two young boys.

The next words were out of my mouth before I could think through them. "What you need is a wife, Pastor."

Miles Jenkins looked at me as if instead of words, a frog had come out of my mouth. "I barely have time for my boys, let alone trying to court someone. And who would marry a widowed pastor with two unruly boys, especially when one of the boys is mute? Thank you, Miss Stuart, for your concern, but I don't really think…"

"Very well," I interrupted. "How about another idea? What if I were to take care of the boys a few days a week for you? I could either do it at your house or at my house. Da won't like it right away, but if the boys will help out some around the farm, I think he could get used to the idea. James and John can teach me more sign language and I can help them with their school work. When their schoolwork is finished, they can help out with whatever needs done." Where had all this come from? Was I crazy? *God, is this You? These boys really need help and so does Pastor Jenkins. Plus it will give me something to do for You. Maybe I can be a surrogate mother to them.*

Pastor Jenkins seemed to be thinking about the idea. He opened and closed his mouth a few times, then looked at each of his boys. James signed something to him in an almost frantic manner. Whatever he said caused his father to crack a smile, the first I remembered seeing from him since I first came to church.

"I guess I know your opinion, James." He turned to John. "What do you think, John?"

John shrugged his shoulders. "It would probably be fine. She's the first person in town to take any interest in understanding James. I'm not sure I like the idea for myself, but it might help James some."

The right side of my mouth curved up. I knew exactly what John needed—hard work.

Pastor Jenkins turned back to me. "I'll pray about it and get back to you in the next couple of days. Would it be all right for me to come out to your place Tuesday evening? It might not happen since I don't know for sure what I will have to do that day."

"That would be fine. Bring the boys, too. You can come for supper. We eat just before dusk."

Pastor Jenkins graced me with another smile. "Sounds like a plan to me."

"Anything to eat something not made by Pa," John said. He seemed to be serious, but I detected a slight teasing tone in his voice. The twinkle in his eye was visible if you looked for it.

I laughed. "I guess it's a plan then?"

"If I can get away in time," Pastor hedged.

"All you have to do is tell people you have dinner plans and the boys won't let you live it down if you don't get to the dinner on time. Right, boys?"

James grinned from ear to ear and nodded his head.

"Yes, ma'am," John said with a grin matching his brothers.

"Sounds like I'll have to make it work somehow," Pastor said with amusement. "We'll see you on Tuesday evening before dusk."

I nodded. "I'll make sure I cook a big meal. Growing boys eat a lot." I winked at James. "Don't work yourself to death, Pastor."

Miles Jenkins laughed. "I'll try not to. God bless you, Miss Stuart."

"God's blessings on you and your family, Pastor Jenkins."

Pastor Jenkins took his youngest son's hand and patted his oldest son's shoulder as he walked to the parsonage.

I turned to go with reluctance. How could I spin this one to Da? Caleb wouldn't mind. At least, I hoped he wouldn't. Da, on the other hand...

As I trudged home, millions of thoughts flooded my mind. I could spin it as a goodwill gesture. Free help on the farm during the summer. Something for me to do. Something to take a deep, vested interest in instead of bothering Da and Caleb so much. A way to finally have some kids to take care of again. Oh, John! Please turn from that budding rebellious spirit before it is too late!

When I walked through the door, Caleb was the only one in the house.

"How was church?" he asked.

"Church was great. The sermon was convicting as always. I realized I haven't been as good of a living example as I should be to you and Da. Caleb, I became a true Christian a few months ago. I realize I haven't been a very good example of that, but I purpose to change this week."

Caleb nodded. "I thought something was different about you. How was the fellowship after church?"

I blinked. He had hardly mentioned what I thought was a life-changing event. I took a quick breath to calm myself. "I actually only talked to three people after church: Pastor Jenkins and his two boys."

Caleb cocked his right eyebrow. "Really? The way you said that makes me think there's a bit of a story there." He straddled a chair and leaned towards me in anticipation.

I chuckled. "There is. It all started as I was walking out of church. I had just reached the bottom of the stairs when two boys almost collided with me. I knew the boys, but not who their parents were. I had them bring me to their da and he turned out to be Pastor Jenkins.

"So I scolded Pastor Jenkins a bit about the behavior of his sons. His response to the scolding was a list of reasons why they run wild. Mainly it's because his wife died two years ago and his work for the church and her people keep him too busy to raise them properly."

"Let me guess," Caleb said, "you offered your services."

"And yours and Da's."

Caleb's eyes widened. "What?" he sputtered.

I smiled. "I think it would be great if John and James could do some work here on the farm. Of course, Pastor Jenkins still has to agree to it. He is going to pray about it and get back to me on Tuesday. Oh, by the way, Pastor Jenkins and his sons will be here for supper on Tuesday."

Caleb's face went blank. "Da won't like that."

"I know. I was hoping you could help me convince him it is for the best. We can have some free farm help this summer. Two young, strong, hard-working boys."

Caleb shook his head. "It might work, but I wouldn't count on it."

"I'll pray about it and take my chances," I said.

I had my opportunity right away as Da walked in.

"Chances with what?" he growled.

I swallowed hard and sent up a quick prayer. "With what I volunteered to do today."

Da narrowed his eyes. "What'd you do now?"

"I invited the Pastor and his two sons over for dinner Tuesday night and I also volunteered to help Pastor Jenkins with his sons. His wife died a couple of years ago and his boys are running wild because Pastor Jenkins is too busy taking care of church business. I suggested we have his sons come here to help us out." I talked fast and with few pauses so Da couldn't interrupt me. "I figured they could help you and Caleb with some of the outdoor work. I'm sure we can figure something out."

Da's narrowed eyes had gradually changed to a glare.

Dear God, I prayed, *please let him agree to at least try it.*

"Keep them out of my way," Da said.

"Don't worry 'bout that, Da," Caleb interjected. "I'll make sure they stay out of your hair."

As Da walked away, Caleb muttered under his breath, "Like I tried to do with Jed."

I shot him a condemning look, but Caleb put on an innocent face and left the room. I took a deep breath and said a prayer of thanks. At least Da and Caleb were okay with my project. Now all I had to do was pray Pastor Jenkins would agree to it.

CHAPTER EIGHT

Tuesday afternoon, I made some of Jed's favorite meals hoping John and James would either like what I made or not be picky. I was about to check on the biscuits when a knock sounded on the door.

I hurried over and opened it. "Pastor Jenkins, John, James. It is good to see you. Come in. I hope you will excuse me, I need to check on the biscuits before I become a decent hostess."

Pastor Jenkins smiled and waved me into the kitchen. "Don't worry about it. We wouldn't want burnt biscuits now, would we Boys?"

James grinned and shook his head while John wrinkled his nose.

"Is there anything we can help with?" Pastor Jenkins asked as he followed me into the kitchen. "Ah, it looks like the table needs to be set. James, would you like to help set the table?"

I turned around in time to see his head bob up and down. I smiled. "I'll tell you where things are as soon as I get these biscuits out of the oven." I bent over the oven and pulled the sheet of biscuits out, putting them on top of the stove.

John came over and was about to hand the basket to me, then changed his mind. "I'll get the biscuits off the sheet. You can go help James set the table."

I laughed. "Yes, Sir! You know, I normally don't allow guests to help in the kitchen, but I knew you wouldn't take no for an answer. Right, Pastor?"

"Correct," Pastor Jenkins said. He seemed less stiff and formal than usual. Maybe it was the homey feel. "And please, while I am a guest in your home, you can call me Miles."

I gave him a sharp look and he must have somehow read my thoughts. Calling him by his first name when we hardly knew each other seemed so irreverent and bold.

He gave me a sheepish smile. "Pastor Jenkins seems too formal for such a casual setting and you said yourself a few months ago that your father and brother don't like to talk about the things of the Lord."

A mischievous grin played across my face. "Okay, I will call you Miles, but only," I pointed a finger at him, "only if you call me Anna."

Miles took a deep bow and answered, "Yes'm, Miz Anna."

John and James burst into laughter and it was only then I remembered John and James had heard every word we had said. My face grew hot as I blushed straight to the roots of my hair.

My only consolation was the look on Miles' face. His was at least as red as mine and his shy, sheepish grin was too endearing. I almost burst out laughing again. Then our eyes met and our embarrassed grins turned into smiles which changed very quickly into contagious laughter.

Everybody stopped laughing abruptly when the back door slammed shut and Da's voice was heard loud and clear, "What's th' meaning of all this caterwauling? Ha' ye gone daft, Anna?"

My spine stiffened and I closed my eyes and mouth against the retort burning in my throat. "No, Da. We were laughing at the fun we were having." I turned to John and James who stared at Da with wide eyes. My heart wept for them. I was sure they had never seen or heard such a reaction from their father. For that matter, they had probably never known anyone who would react in such a way. *Lord, is it right to expose them to Da?*

Turning my thoughts away from Da, I spoke to James and John. "Are the biscuits all in the basket?"

John nodded as he tore his eyes away from Da. The back door opened again and Caleb stepped into the kitchen.

"Ah, our guests arrived before we were done in the barn. So sorry for our inhospitality, but cows and horses wait for no man." He turned to Miles. "You must be Pastor Jenkins." Stepping closer and moving around Da, he held out his hand. "A pleasure to meet you, Sir. I'm Caleb Stuart. I'm sure Anna's told you all about me." He winked at John and James. "Just like she's told me all about you and your two boys."

Miles shook Caleb's hand. "Please call me Miles." The corners of his mouth acted like they wanted to smile. "And Anna has told the boys some things about you, though nothing too terrible as of

95

yet, from what they have told me."

The ever-serious Pastor had a mischievous side to him? I never would've guessed that. I checked the table and saw it was set. "Dinner is served, Gentlemen. Please take your seats."

James touched my arm to get my attention. He signed a question to me, but I couldn't read it. I looked at John to see if he had caught what his brother had said, but before John could open his mouth, Miles came to his rescue.

"That is a good question, James. Do you have assigned seats, Anna?"

I smiled. "No, we don't. You may sit on any of the chairs." I looked up at Caleb and winked at him. "I don't suggest sitting on the table, though."

James grinned and signed something else.

"Where am I sitting? Wherever there is a seat available, I suppose," I replied to his question.

His hands moved quickly again while I watched intently.

"What?" My eyebrows drew together in confusion.

Miles cleared his throat a few times before interpreting for his son. "He wants you to sit between him and myself." Miles looked across the room to Caleb and Da. "If that's all right with you, Mr. Stuart."

Da stared Miles down for a few seconds. "My daughter can sit where she likes."

"I guess it's settled then," Caleb said, patting his stomach. "I don't know 'bout you boys, but I'm starved!"

Chairs scraped against the wood floors as everybody sat down. Before I had a chance to pull my chair out, I got the surprise of my life when James pulled it out for me and held onto the back looking at me expectantly. I sat down and he tried to scoot the chair in, but it was too heavy for the boy. I was about to finish scooting myself in when Miles pushed his chair back, stood up, and scooted my chair in for me.

I sat there for a few seconds, in shock, looking between father and son. I had never been treated this way before.

I suddenly caught sight of Da's expression. It was something between a glare and admiration. Then he started dishing up his food. I closed my eyes. I had forgotten to warn the Jenkins men that Da and Caleb didn't say a blessing before their meals. Opening my eyes, I dared a sidelong glance at Miles.

The look on his face was unreadable, almost as if he was trying to decide whether or not to pray. I saw the second he made up his mind. He bowed his head and folded his hands.

"Lord in heaven," he prayed, "we come to you this evening to thank You for Your bountiful care. Bless the hands that prepared this food and bless those who provided the food for us. Bless this food to our bodies and give us uplifting conversation during our meal. Thank You for sending Your Son to die for us and for giving us a sunny day in which to serve You. In Jesus' name I pray, Amen."

When I opened my eyes after the prayer, I chose not to look across the table at Da and Caleb, instead I concentrated on dishing up the food in front of me.

Miles was the first to speak after the food had all been passed around and dished up. "Mr. Stuart,

I noticed on the way here that you have a good-sized corn field. Do you sell it in town or use it all for your animals and re-seeding?"

Da grunted. "Call me Iain. I ain't been called 'Mr. Stuart' for years. I sell some corn, but keep most of it."

I could see John practically bouncing up and down in his chair. "Do you shell it first?" he asked. "How do you harvest it? When is the best time to plant?"

Caleb laughed. "Miles, do you have a budding farmer on your hands?"

Miles quirked an eyebrow. "It would appear so." He turned to his eldest son. "I didn't know you were so interested in farming."

John shrugged. "Is someone going to answer my questions?"

Caleb's eyes twinkled. Knowing him, he loved the idea of having someone to talk to about farming. "Sure. We plant in the spring, right after the last frost. Harvesting is best done during the Harvest Moon in September. As for shelling, it depends on who we sell the corn to. Sometimes we do, sometimes we don't. Da was able to buy a sheller last year, so we no longer have to ruin our hands to do it ourselves."

I watched as Caleb answered many more questions from John. At one point during the two-way conversation, Miles' eyes met mine and we both smiled at John's obvious connection with Caleb.

"I think John has found a new friend," I said.

Miles nodded. "He certainly has." He turned to look toward his son. His eyes teared up suddenly and he swallowed. "I had no idea John had an interest in farming."

I was about to respond when James tugged on my sleeve. I turned to him and was soon lost in a silent conversation with the younger Jenkins boy.

Even though it was dark, John and James went outside with Caleb after dinner to look at the farm. I smiled at their enthusiasm. Even Caleb seemed to enjoy having the boys around. Da on the other hand went sullenly about his evening chores and retired to bed.

Miles helped me clear the table despite all my protests. "Don't you want to go out with your boys and see the farm?"

Miles laughed and nodded toward the window. "It's dark, Anna. There isn't anything to see except the animals. I've seen farm animals many times in my life. I don't think I'll miss much this time. And I happen to know I will get a full report as soon as we head back home."

I cocked my head and gave a small smile. "I suppose."

I poured the hot water from the pan on the stove into the dishpan and started washing the dishes.

Miles leaned his back against the counter and cleared his throat. "Besides, I wanted to talk to you without the boys around."

I cocked an eyebrow while I gave the plate my full attention. "Oh?"

"What are your thoughts for this..." he waved a hand in the air, "...whatever you want to call it?"

I took a deep breath and let it out slowly. "Well, I thought perhaps they could come out here a couple days a week and I could go to your place the other days. That way your house can get a good cleaning and you three can eat a few decent meals." I flashed a mischievous grin at him.

Miles chuckled as he turned around and helped dry the dishes. "Do you want set days or decide from week-to-week?"

I thought while I washed and rinsed the rest of the plates. "Well, Saturdays would probably be a good day for them to be here." I saw Miles' head bob up and down. "Maybe you could join us for dinner on Tuesday evenings?"

Miles dried the plate he was holding until I thought he might rub the finish off. "That's a possibility."

"Perhaps we could tentatively set up Tuesdays, Thursdays, and Saturdays here and Mondays, Wednesdays, and Fridays at your place." I paused in my dish washing. "Actually, that works well. I do laundry on Monday and my normal baking days are Tuesday and Wednesday. I can bake for us on Tuesdays and at your place on Wednesdays. Hmmm..."

"You sound like you've got it all worked out."

I laughed. "Not even close. I may have some of it kind of figured out, but definitely not all of it."

"It sounds like a plan to me, anyway. I'll make sure the boys know what they're doing."

I nodded.

Miles dried two more plates before he spoke

again. "How has your personal Bible study been? Actually, let me rephrase that. Have you run across anything that you would like me to try to answer?"

I kept my eyes on the dishwater as I swished the rag across the pan. "Bible memorization. How important is it and how do your boys memorize so quickly?"

Miles took a deep breath. "Bible memorization is very important. I wish more of my parishioners would start memorizing. The Bible has many verses about hiding God's Word in your heart. One of the most well-known is Psalm 119:11, 'Thy word have I hid in mine heart, that I might not sin against thee.'

"As for my boys, they have a natural bent toward memorizing. If they have a special method, I don't know it, but you could always ask them."

"I might just do that," I replied. "There, that's the last of the dishes," I announced in triumph.

"Hallelujah!" Miles said with a grin.

I held out the dishrag. "'Here, you can wash the table off while I put these dishes away."

Miles took the dishrag between his thumb and forefinger. "Are you always this bossy with your guests?"

"No, not really. You're just too easy to boss around. And we don't have many guests."

Miles gave me a look of disbelief and I laughed.

"What?" I asked. "Nobody's ever told you that before?"

Miles shook his head. His brown hair brushed along his forehead and almost reached his raised eyebrows.

"Really?" I was incredulous. Was I the only

one who was brave enough—or stupid enough—to tease and boss around the pastor?

"Really," Miles said. "Rebekah, my wife, said I was the bossy one. I was the one who was always teasing others. She also said I never let anyone boss me around or tease me."

"Maybe it's because I'm the only one bold enough to do that to a pastor."

Miles shrugged and washed off the table.

While I put the dishes away, I said, "You really should go see the farm with the boys…"

"And leave you here alone to finish cleaning up?" Miles interrupted. "I don't think so. You had twice as many dishes to do because we came over."

"I was the one who invited you, remember?"

Miles shrugged. "I still feel bad that you've got extra work because of us."

I turned away from the cupboards where I had been hiding. "Miles Jenkins," I scolded, "You have a church to shepherd, you are trying to be both mother and father to two rambunctious boys, and you are doing all of this with no wife or housekeeper to feed you, clothe you, and clean for you. I only have two grown farm boys to cook for, clean up after, and clothe. They can spare me."

I took a step closer to Miles and looked him straight in the eye. "Ever since I became a Christian, I have been praying for a ministry opportunity. I've been praying for some way to serve my community, the church, or any other way possible. When your boys nearly ran me over and I found out they were motherless, I knew God had answered my prayers. Don't you dare take this away from me!"

Miles backed away from me a step and his

Adam's apple bobbed as he swallowed. He held his hands up in surrender. "I can see you are a formidable woman." He chewed his bottom lip. "That will be good for John and James."

I felt the corners of my mouth twitch as I tried not to smile. "What about for you?"

Miles narrowed his eyes at me before letting a grin spread across his face. "Yeah." He let his hands fall along his sides. "I suppose it might be good for me, too."

I was about to say something, but the words flew right out of my brain when the kitchen door slammed shut and two pairs of feet came racing through the kitchen.

I stepped around Pastor Jenkins and confronted the culprits. "Rule number one in this house is to never slam the doors. Whether you are opening them or closing them, always, always do so gently. My da is in his bedroom right now trying to get to sleep. But even if he was outside, you should still close the door gently. The rougher you handle the door, the more likely it will be to need fixing. And believe me, you do not want to have to replace, or fix, that door. You hear me?"

John and James stared at me with huge eyes and nodded their heads in agreement.

"Good." I let the stern look leave my face. "Now then, what did you two get into outside?" I looked over their heads at my brother. He had a twinkle in his eyes that could mean most anything, but the smile on his face said he had enjoyed his evening.

"We got to feed the cows and the horses and the chickens. Caleb said the chickens are usually your job, but since you had extra dishes we may's well take care of it for you." John took a breath before continuing. "Then Mr. Caleb showed us the corn, wheat, barley and…and…" He turned to look at Caleb. "What was the other stuff called?"

Caleb cleared his throat in what seemed to me to be an attempt at swallowing down his laughter. "The rye?"

"That's what it was. Rye and hay. They harvest the hay three or four times a year and use it mostly in the winter to feed the animals. In the summer the animals can eat the grass. The rest of the crops are only harvested in the fall since they don't ripen but the once."

Miles cleared his throat and gave John a look that should have shut him up, but he kept going.

"Next time we come out…We are coming out again, aren't we, Pa?"

"Yes, you will be. We can talk about it on our way home."

John's eyes lit up with excitement and James came closer to me and gave me a small hug. "Really, Pa?"

Miles smiled. "Really. Now, I think we'd best get home. We have a lot of work to do tomorrow."

"Aww, Pa!" John protested. "Do we have to?"

Miles sighed. "Yes, John, we do. Farmers have to get up really early in the morning, which means they have to go to bed earlier than us city folks." Miles looked up at me and winked.

I fought against a giggle and squatted down to James' level. We exchanged a short conversation about how he had liked the farm. He had loved it, though he wasn't quite as much in love with it as his brother was. Maybe, just maybe, he wouldn't mind helping me with some of the inside work and working in the garden.

As I recalled the conversations I'd had with John and James, I remembered the story of Jacob and Esau. Jacob liked staying close to home, while Esau was a wanderer and hunter. *Lord, keep John from turning out like Esau did.*

It took a combination effort from Miles and me to push John out the door and down the road toward town.

I watched the three Jenkins men until they reached the road and I could no longer see them.

"You're really going to help 'em out?" Caleb asked as he leaned against the door frame behind me.

"Yes, I am," I said. "Are you?" I turned around to look at Caleb.

He took a deep breath. "It was nice having those two boys around. It reminded me of when Jed would follow my every move. Every time I turned around to see John watching me with awestruck eyes, Jed's face would flash into my memory." He paused for a few seconds. "Yes, I'll help 'em while they're out here. John anyway. If I wanna help James, I'll have to learn that fancy hand signing." He grinned. "I'm not sure I can learn it fast enough for him."

I laughed. "No, probably not. I don't think James will be out with you much anyway. Next time he comes, I'll probably get him to help me inside."

Caleb nodded. "Of the two, I think he's the one who most craves a mother's love. You'll be good at that."

Tears sprang to my eyes. "Are you sure?"

Caleb looked startled and stood up straight. "Of course I am. Why would you think you wouldn't be?"

I hugged my arms to my chest. "Jed ran off despite my care."

Caleb growled. "That was Da's doin', not yours. He probably would've run off years earlier if it hadn't been for you."

My chest felt tight and I had a hard time getting my breath to come. "You really think so?"

Caleb took two steps toward me and folded me into his arms. He kissed the top of my head. "Yes, Baby Sister, I do. I really do."

I clenched my fists and tried to fight for control over these overwhelming feelings, but it didn't work and I sobbed in his arms until there was nothing left in me. When my sobbing slowed, Caleb kept an arm around me and led me back into the house, up the stairs, and to my room.

"Sleep well, Anna. Dream pleasant dreams about little James and John."

I tried to give a short laugh, but it came out more like a strangled cry. "I'll try. Thank you for everything, Caleb."

He tousled my hair. "You're welcome, Little Sister."

He stepped away from the door and walked to his own room. I closed my door and leaned against it, trying to collect my thoughts, my grief, my joy, my…everything really.

"God, I can't do this on my own. Help me to lean on You. I know Da and Caleb must be grieving too, but they hide it so well. I know I can't do this while I feel like I'm the only one grieving. Help me, Lord!"

CHAPTER NINE

The next morning, I made breakfast for Da and Caleb, ate mine and cleaned up before heading over to the parsonage. Today would be evaluation day.

I knocked on the front door when I arrived. The pounding of two pairs of feet raced from inside. When the door opened there were two grinning, happy faces framed in the doorway. "Good morning, John and James."

"Let her inside, you two," a deeper male voice commanded. I could hear the smile in his voice, although I couldn't see him.

John and James both scurried out of my way and I stepped into the parsonage for the first time. As I looked around, I was surprised how clean it really was. The floors had been swept in the last week and there was very little clutter around. I hoped the kitchen looked this good.

Miles' voice interrupted my thoughts. "Do you have any questions before I leave?"

"Discipline," I said. "We never discussed what I should do if they misbehave."

Miles nodded his head. "Most likely that will be when, not if. What do you think boys? How should Miss Stuart punish you if you misbehave?"

John stared at his father. "You actually want our opinion?"

Miles chuckled. "I was teasing you. How about you two go into the kitchen and clean up breakfast while we talk?" He phrased it as a question, but it was more of a command.

"Yes, Pa," John said. James gave a quick nod and both of them trudged toward the back of the house.

"Now," Miles said, "I think the best thing would be for you to sit them down, tell them what they did wrong and have them tell me when I get home. Then I will punish them."

I nodded slowly. "Yes, I think that will work very well."

"Good, then I will get off to church and leave you to whatever it is you need to do."

"There is one more thing, Miles," I said. "I am going to go through your house and evaluate what is needed, especially for clothes and food. Shall I leave a list of what you need?"

"Yes, then I can look it over and you can get the supplies on Friday."

"I will do that. Have a good day at work."

Grief flashed in his eyes before he turned and walked out the door. Did I say something wrong? I didn't have time to think about it before dishes clattered to the floor. I sighed. Boys in the kitchen. This should be a fun day.

After our minor catastrophe with a broken plate, the day calmed down a little. I got them sent off to school with a sack lunch and then went through all of the boys' clothes and found some things that were in desperate need of replacement. When that was done, I ate a quick lunch and went through the pantry.

The pantry wasn't too bad considering it had been three young men here for over two years. They were low on some essentials, but all in all, it was halfway decent. No canned goods, but that didn't surprise me in the least. Our garden harvest would be more than enough to supply both households. *Thank You, Lord, for my seeming insanity this spring when I planted twice as much in the garden as I should have. Now I know why; because You knew I would need it.*

I reorganized the pantry and finished writing out the list of things that would be needed. When the list was done, I gave myself a thorough tour of the house, taking stock of what rooms needed the most scrubbing down and which rooms could wait. The living room was the first to be done. I decided to wait until John and James got home. Once they were finished with their homework, I could get them to help me with the scrubbing, beating the rugs, dusting, and sweeping. Meanwhile, I would get supper put together.

By the time John and James crashed through the door, I had a batch of cookies cooling on the table, stew on the stove, and cornbread ready to go in the oven.

Four feet scurried through the house as the two boys put their school books away and then rushed into the kitchen.

"Are those cookies?" John asked, surprise in his voice.

I turned around with a grin. "Yes, they are. Has it really been that long since you had cookies?"

"Naw, we get some at church dinners, but not for after school snacks."

"Who said they were for your snack?" I teased.

James' eyes grew wide and he put his thumb and fingers together and moved them to his mouth while shaking his head with a confused look on his face.

I laughed. "I was teasing your brother, James. They are for snack today and dessert tonight, and whenever else your pa lets you have some."

"Yippee!!" John squealed as he rushed to the table.

"Only one for snack," I ordered. "We don't want you to spoil your dinner." They each took a cookie. "Now, do either of you have any homework?"

"Not very much," John said with a mouthful of oatmeal cookie.

"Chew and swallow before you speak, young man."

John chewed and gulped down the bite of sugary sweetness. "Yes, ma'am. I don't have very much homework. Pa usually has us do it after supper."

"Well, how about we see if you can do your homework now and then you can have some time to play games or something with your pa after supper instead of doing homework," I suggested.

"Really? You think Pa would do that?"

James clapped his hands together and glared at

his brother. "Of course he would," James signed. "Pa only has us do it after supper, so he can help us if we need help. Miss Stuart can help us now that she's taking care of us."

I smiled and looked over at John. John was flushed. "Right, I hadn't thought of that. Okay." He ran out of the room and came back with his and James' school books. "Here ya go, James."

I cleared my throat and John looked at me. "What?"

"Try saying that again, this time with a proper use of your personal pronoun."

"Huh?" John's face clouded up with confusion.

"He, she, it, you, your, his, hers, and they, are all personal pronouns. Use the correct pronoun in your sentence."

"Oh. I shoulda said 'Here YOU go, James."

"Yes, and 'shoulda' should have been 'should've'."

John wrinkled up his nose. "Sometimes I wish I was mute like James. Then I wouldn't have to worry so much about proper grammar."

I chuckled. "It's good to learn anyway, John. Now, you two get started on your homework and if you have any questions, I'll be cleaning up in the living room."

"Yes, ma'am," John said as James' head bobbed up and down.

Half an hour later, John and James joined me in the living room. "Everything done?" I asked.

"Yep. What're we going to do next?" John asked.

"I would like to get this room thoroughly cleaned. So, we need to beat the rugs, dust, scrub the walls, and sweep the floors. And it needs to be done in that order. I was thinking you two could beat the rugs while I dust, then we can let them air out while we all scrub the walls together. How does that sound?"

The ear to ear grins on both faces gave me all the answer I needed. Together, we took the rugs outside and hung them on the clothesline. Then John and James left in search of sturdy sticks while I took a rag and removed as much of the dust in the room as I could. I finished first and went out to see how they were doing. What I saw when I got outside brought a smile to my face.

John and James stood on either side of the rug, stick in hand while John chanted out the rhythm. First one boy would hit the rug, then the other in perfect rhythm. I wished for some way to capture this moment so Miles could see it. Not wanting them to know I had been watching them, I sneaked back into the house and gathered rags and three bowls of soapy water and started moving the furniture away from the walls.

The last chair barely had time to settle on all four legs when laughter came toward me from the kitchen. "Well, we beat those rugs into submission, Miss Stuart," John said. "They revealed all their dirt and got rid of it."

The three of us burst into laughter at his almost-serious statement. By the time we stopped laughing, we each had tears streaming down our faces.

"Oh, John, you are funny," I gasped. "What do you say to starting on the walls?"

"Sounds great!" John exclaimed. "Where shall we start, General?"

I put on my most serious face and looked them each up and down. "Private John, you take that bowl and two rags and start where that stool is. Once I am done on my stool, you will get on the stool and start as high as you can reach. Private James, you take that bowl and two rags and start where Private John leaves off. Understood?"

"Aye, aye, Sir! Er, ma'am." John saluted and I chuckled again. As we scrubbed the walls, John and I sang as many hymns as we could think of. As I scrubbed the last wall, there was a lull in the singing as we both ran out of ideas. Suddenly, one came to mind and I sang:

Rop tú mo baile, a Choimdiu cride:
ní ní nech aile acht Rí secht nime.
Rop tú mo scrútain i l-ló 's i n-aidche;
rop tú ad-chëar im chotlud caidche.

I finished my part of the scrubbing before I was done with the hymn, but I kept singing as I watched the boys conclude their scrubbing. By the time the last note faded, John and James were done with their scrubbing and stood watching me.

"That was beautiful," a deep voice behind me said.

I jumped and put a hand over my heart. "Pastor Jenkins, when did you get back?"

"Just in time to hear an angel singing in an unknown language," he said with a smile.

"And who might that be?" I asked, cocking an eyebrow.

"What song and language was that, anyway?" Miles asked, ignoring my question.

"Me mither's favorite hymn in her native

113

tongue: The Gaelic version of 'Be Thou My Vision'," I said with an air of mock haughtiness and in an Irish accent—I liked to switch intermittently between my mama's native accent and my da's.

Miles cocked an eyebrow at me and smiled. "It looks nice in here."

"I couldn't have done it without John and James helping me out," I said.

"Pa," John exclaimed. "Can we do something fun tonight? We've already got our homework finished."

Miles chuckled. "It sounds like we could." When John looked about ready to ask another question, Miles held up his hand. "Let me talk to Anna first and send her on her way home. Then we can talk about everything you did today." He looked at the clock. "You two go get washed up for supper and set the table."

"Yes, Pa," John said.

James gave his da a hug as he passed by.

"How did it go?" Miles asked me as they walked out the door.

"Way too fast. I left you a list on the table. There are a few food items you are low on and the boys' clothes are starting to get rather worn. Before Friday, could you find some time to go through yours so I know what you might need as well?"

Miles nodded. "I can do that. Nothing that needs to be reported?"

I shook my head. "No, I think they were too excited about having me here to make trouble or get into trouble. Give them a couple of weeks. When the newness wears off, then they'll start being trouble. Oh, and there's cornbread in the oven that should be done in a few minutes."

"You're probably right. Thank you, Anna." He held out his hand to me and I put mine in his and shook it.

"You're welcome," I said.

Miles stepped aside and I walked past him and out the door to go feed my hungry men.

Thursday seemed to creep by while I cleaned our home and waited for school to be let out. Then it flew. After charging through our front door, John and James literally stuffed their snack into their mouths and John ran out to the fields to help with whatever Caleb concocted for him to do in the barn. James and I looked at what still needed to be planted for our fall crop.

As I evaluated what needed planting when, I realized the garden needed to be weeded. A smile formed on my lips. Weeding was the perfect Saturday chore for two energetic boys.

All too soon, I saw the time had come for the boys to head home. "James, go find your brother and tell him it is time to go home, please."

"Yes, ma'am," he signed.

After the boys were on their way, I finished planning our Saturday weeding before I went inside to fix some cornbread, beans, and apple pie for Da and Caleb.

After evening chores, Caleb sat down at the table for one last piece of apple pie.

"How did John do?" I asked.

Caleb looked up at me and shook his head. "That boy is smart and fast. I couldn't believe how quickly he got the harnesses done. And he did a great job on them. If he weren't so young and we had enough money, I'd hire him. And he is always asking questions about farming and harvesting and planting and things like that."

I threw my head back and laughed. "I'm not surprised."

"How was James?" Caleb asked as he put the last bit of pie in his mouth.

"He was really quiet today."

"Isn't he always quiet?" I could tell Caleb was confused.

"Yes, but he usually at least talks to me with his hands. Granted, I kept him busy weeding, but he still seemed...I'm not really sure what to call it. More subdued, maybe?"

"He might need some time to get used to the idea of having a woman around again. It's been two years and he was pretty young when his mama died."

I nodded. "That's probably what it is. Oh! I almost forgot. Do you have any plans for the boys on Saturday?"

"No. Why?"

"I would like them to help with the weeding. I've neglected it this week and it is starting to get out of hand."

Caleb grinned. "Anything so I don't have to."

I put a hand on my hip. "And here I thought I could use you as a good example for them and have you show them what to do."

Caleb stood up and held his hands in the air.

116

"Nope. Nothin' doin'. You want them to do it, you can show 'em how it's done. I'm going to bed now. See you in the morning."

I laughed as Caleb beat a hasty retreat up the stairs. *Brothers,* I thought as I cleaned up Caleb's plate and headed to my own bed.

Friday was similar to Wednesday except that instead of going through clothes in the morning, I spent the morning shopping for material and food. I bought flour, butter, lard, sugar and the material needed for new shirts. The total I spent—with Pastor Jenkins' money—was actually less than either of us were anticipating; only $1.70 instead of the $2.00 I was anticipating.

After school, the boys finished their homework and we scrubbed the kitchen down. The Jenkins men would have a cold supper, but it would be in an extra clean kitchen and at least two of them didn't care as long as their da wasn't doing the cooking.

The kitchen was clean, the table was set and supper was on the table. Pastor Jenkins wasn't home when I left, but I had to get home or my da and Caleb would be grumping that their supper wasn't ready. I left the boys with careful instructions on how to behave and what to do before their da got home.

When I stepped outside, I took a deep breath and worked up the energy to walk home. I couldn't wait until their house was scrubbed so I could get on with some of the normal chores for once.

Chores like bread baking and doing the laundry. Chores I used to dislike.

As soon as breakfast was cleaned up on Saturday, I gathered a wheelbarrow, two hoes, string, and four sturdy sticks. I pushed the wheelbarrow full of items to the garden. After I took a quick scan of the rows, I grabbed the sticks and string out of the wheelbarrow.

I walked a third of the way along the garden edge and put a stick in the ground. I then attached the string to the stick and walked across the garden. When I reached the other side, I put another stick in the ground and attached the string. Once it was tied securely, I pulled my jackknife out of the pocket in my skirt and cut the string. After that was done, I repeated the process.

As I cut the string for the third, and last, time, the sound of John chattering away to his brother reached my ears and walked to the road to meet them.

"What's the plan today?" John yelled when he saw me.

I waited until they were closer before I answered. "Weeding. Today, gentlemen, we shall have a contest to see who can weed the fastest and best."

John grimaced. "Weeding? Yuck!"

I turned to look at James. His eyes sparkled and his mouth curved upward into an excited grin.

"The sooner we get started, the sooner we can be done."

While we weeded, I tried to keep at least a little conversation going. It was hard though, because I had the feeling I was leaving James out since he couldn't weed and talk at the same time.

"How do you boys memorize Scripture so well?"

"We work together on it," John said as he pulled some grass out of the potatoes. "We read the verse out loud together...Well, as best we can with James doing sign language instead. Then we alternate days we start quoting. For example, it was my turn to start today. After we read the verse, I looked it over a couple of times, then I tried to quote it from memory. If I messed up or couldn't remember the next word, James would tell me what it was. When I was done, James quoted it."

"So you work on it together? How do you decide what to memorize?" I asked.

James clapped his hands for my attention. He was almost buried as he knelt among the nearly half-grown corn. "We each take turns choosing a chapter or verse to learn," he signed.

I nodded and returned to my weeding, thoughtful and quiet. How was I supposed to do that when I didn't have someone to help me memorize?

We took a quick break to eat lunch. After lunch, I gave each of the boys a straw hat to wear to protect their faces from the hot sun. Then we headed back to the garden to finish the weeding.

As suppertime approached, Caleb came to the garden to find out how we were doing. John pulled his last weed and bounced over to Caleb. "Look what we did!" he exclaimed. "We've got the whole garden weeded! I didn't like doing it, but I tried to

119

do my best."

Caleb looked at the garden. "That's pretty impressive for first-time garden weeders."

John had a look on his face that said he was about to talk our ears off. "You two need to get back home fast or your father will be coming here to find out what happened to you."

John grinned. "Okay, let's stay here, James."

James grinned and nodded his head. "I want to stay and I want Pa to come, too," he signed.

I shook my head and looked at Caleb with an appeal in my eyes.

"Don't look at me," he said. "If I had my way, I'd let 'em stay, too."

I scowled at him and he quickly backed up in surrender. "On the other hand, Da and Miles probably wouldn't like it. How about I walk you two home?" Caleb asked.

"YES!" John shouted.

John and James both said hurried goodbyes and ran out to the road, dragging Caleb behind them.

CHAPTER TEN

The churchyard was full of people when I turned off the road the next Sunday. I scanned the yard for James and John, but couldn't see them. My heart sank a couple inches when I saw the busybody of the church headed my way with a resolute step. In desperation, I looked around for anyone else to talk to, but didn't see anybody I knew well enough to walk up to and start talking to them.

"Anna Stuart, how nice to see you," the woman enthused.

"Mrs. Morgan." I pasted a smile onto my face. I was sure she could see right through my mask of politeness. "How are you this fine morning?"

"I'm fine. I'm fine. I really came over here to find out what you have been doing at Pastor Jenkins' house."

I stared at Mrs. Morgan. "What do you mean?"

"I mean exactly what I said. What do you do over there?"

"I take care of John and James, give them the attention they have been lacking for over two years, clean the house, do the laundry, and cook a few meals. I'm doing what any decent woman, with a little extra time on her hands, should do. I saw a widower with two young boys struggling to balance his home and work life and keep both of them running smoothly. In case you hadn't noticed, both the church and the boys have struggled ever since Miles Jenkins' wife died. All I'm doing is trying to help them out as best I can."

Mrs. Morgan narrowed her eyes. "Uh-huh. Don't try to fool me, young lady. I know a woman in love when I see one."

"Excuse me?" I was indignant. I took a few seconds to look around and see who was nearby. Nobody was near enough to hear. *God, help me stop this woman from believing these things. Please!*

Mrs. Morgan's voice broke into my prayer. "I've seen those puppy eyes of yours."

I straightened my back, clenched my jaw, and replied in a rather sharp tone. "Yes, you have. But, only when I've been looking at James and John, not their father. He is a nice man who would make any young lady a wonderful husband, but I am not the type of woman who throws herself at any man, no matter how old and spinsterish I get. Not to mention the fact that I barely know him. I am most assuredly not a good candidate for a Pastor's wife and I will be the first to admit that. I am short-tempered, easily riled, and much too controlling to be any good as 'the leading woman' in the community." I paused to take a deep breath and tried to calm my rising anger. "Now, if you will excuse me, I need to go somewhere to prepare myself for worshiping the Lord."

As I turned away from the astonished widow, a small hand slipped into mine and tugged me toward the road. I looked down and James motioned me away from the church and into the woods.

Allowing him to lead me away, we came to a faint path leading into the trees. Less than a minute later, we arrived in a small clearing. James led me to a pair of stumps and motioned for me to sit down on one. He sat on the other stump, facing me.

Using sign language, he explained to me that this spot was where he and his da went when they wanted to disappear for awhile to talk without distractions. After the explanation, he stood up and asked if I could find my way back on my own.

With tears welling in my eyes, I nodded to him, put the fingers of my open palm to my chin briefly before moving it away from my body. While making the motion, I mouthed the words, "Thank you." Too overcome for speech, I was suddenly very grateful I could speak to this sweet boy using signs. James had been gone for mere seconds before I cried out to God. After a few minutes in prayer, I felt like I was ready to enter the Lord's house. As I emerged from the woods, a smile formed on my face at the sight of two little gentlemen watching the path very closely. James ran to me and signed to ask if I was feeling better.

"Yes, I am. Thank you for your concern."

John walked up to me looking like his father, a concerned frown on his face. "James told me what happened and we agreed Pa should be told about it. After all, it does affect him and reflect on his reputation as well." He took a deep breath. "I also think you should be there to tell him. Since you were the one she was speakin' to and all."

It took all my concentration not to stare at John. Where had this serious young man come from? What had he done with the fun-loving, carefree boy? I shook myself mentally. John was at the age where boy and man were fighting each other for dominance.

"We will wait until after church. It's about to start and we should get inside."

James and John both nodded and the three of us walked into the church together.

Mrs. Morgan was sitting in my line of vision all throughout church and I had a hard time concentrating on the service. I honestly cannot tell you what was sung, read, or preached about that day. My mind raced with the things Mrs. Morgan had said. How many others thought that way? I also prayed for wisdom on telling Miles…Pastor Jenkins…and for dealing with whatever might come up as a result. Not to mention searching my own heart for any wrong motives I might have for helping Miles.

I was so distracted by my own internal prayers, I didn't realize church was done until I felt like I was being watched. I lifted my head and turned it from side to side. James and John flanked me and were staring at me.

James signed, "Are you coming?" at the same time John asked, "Are you okay?"

I made a fist and nodded it up and down in James' direction before I turned to face John. I took a deep breath, held it for a few seconds and then let it out. "Yes, I am fine, John. I was just praying."

John smiled grimly and turned to leave the pew. I stood up and followed him out of the pew and out of the church. I shook Mil...Pastor Jenkins' hand as he stood at the door, and before I could say anything, John said, "Pa, the three of us need to talk to you when you're done here."

Pastor Jenkins raised an eyebrow in my direction and I decided to simply give him a nod. John, James, and I moved away from the crowd of churchgoers and stood together in silence until Pastor Jenkins joined us.

When Pastor Jenkins came over to us after doing his obligatory fellowship, John took matters into his own hands again. "Mrs. Morgan thinks Miss Stuart wants to become our stepmom."

At John's outburst, I turned my eyes to watch Pastor Jenkins. I saw a plethora of emotions flit across his face: anger, surprise, shock, amazement. Then he swallowed hard and seemed to choke on his next word, "What?"

I stepped in and told him the whole thing, ending with "...and the boys thought you should know. After they said as much, I agreed with them."

Pastor Jenkins looked away at the emptying churchyard and heaved a sigh. "If...no, when, Mrs. Morgan gets around to telling this to others in the community, you and I will both have some people who shun us. Especially you."

I shrugged. "That's not a big deal. I'm used to being talked about and being alone." The left corner of my mouth curled up slightly at the expression on his face. "I practically raised my youngest brother from infancy until he left at age fourteen. Because of this, I had very few friends since I could never stay after school. By the time Jed left, I was twenty-three and already a spinster. Nobody wants to be friends with a spinster."

"I do," John said with conviction.

I smiled at him. "Thank you John." I looked over at the increasingly uncomfortable Pastor Jenkins. "You don't have to say anything, Pastor. As hard as it was, it all worked out for the best. If it hadn't been for all those years alone, I never would've been able to accept Christ for who He is."

Pastor Jenkins looked at me with quizzical eyes. "What do you mean by that?"

"Seven years ago, I would never have reacted the way I did to the letter Jed sent me about being a Christian. I thought I was a good enough Christian on my own merit whether I went to church or not. I was too sure of myself, too confident in being able to hold everything together by myself. When the letter did finally come—almost exactly seven years after Jed left—I was tired of the life I was living and tired of trying to keep everything together.

"Then I read the letter and my heart broke." Tears welled up in my eyes and I looked away from Pastor Jenkins only to just miss meeting the tear-filled eyes of James. James saw my tears and ran up to me, putting his small arms around my waist. I put my hands on his shoulders and took a deep breath before continuing. "I was nine when Jed was born and Mama died. I pretty much raised Jed single-handedly and felt very motherly and possessive of him. When we got the letter about his death, I went through a week of barely surviving.

"Then Wilma came over and invited me to church. I decided to give it another try. Then another and another. Your sermons and what I was reading in the Bible were the only things that kept me from going into melancholy."

Throughout my whole explanation, I had avoided eye contact with anybody. At the end, I finally let my gaze flit to Miles' face. His eyes were closed and he had a concerned, sympathetic look on his face. He must have felt me looking at him because by the time I registered the look, his eyes were open and I looked away from him.

When Pastor Jenkins spoke, his voice was just above a whisper. "Anna, I am sorry for your loss. I had no idea you had struggled so much with it. As for what Mrs. Morgan thinks, maybe ignoring the rumors will be enough to show them you aren't trying to needle your way into my heart." His voice grew a little stronger and a finger pulled my chin up. I jerked away from him, my eyes darting around the deserted churchyard. I breathed a sigh of relief when I saw that nobody was around.

Pastor Jenkins' eyebrows furrowed. "Why are you so jumpy today, Anna?"

"Mrs. Morgan already thinks I have ulterior motives for taking care of James and John. We don't need to give her any more ideas." I took a step backward and James let go of me with a puzzled look on his face.

Pastor Jenkins tensed. "You think they would really think that?"

"Think what, Pa?" John asked.

Pastor Jenkins sent his son a look that told

him to keep quiet. "Boys, go back to the house and start lunch," he ordered.

John's face fell, but he and James slowly moved off to do as his father had said.

As soon as they were in the house, I looked the pastor full in the face. "Yes, they would think that."

Pastor Jenkins shifted his feet and clenched his jaw. "I never thought of that. I assumed everybody knew I would never do something like that or allow anybody I didn't trust into my home."

I nodded. "I agree and I think most of them would realize that, but some of them don't."

Pastor Jenkins looked down at me. "Was she more upset with you or me?"

My laugh had a slight bitter sound to it. "Definitely with me. I'm the intruder on her perfect plans. I'm the one with the evil plans to snare you into marrying me." I pointed at myself. "Me, the worst possible candidate to be a wife, let alone a pastor's wife."

He fought a smile and cocked an eyebrow. "That sounds like a challenge, Miss Stuart."

"What do you mean?"

"I think you would be a good 'candidate' for a wife to someone. We just have to figure out for whom." He had a mischievous glint in his eyes I did not like.

I backed up a few steps and shook my head, but before I could speak, he interrupted me. "As for Mrs. Morgan, I will have to do something about that. There is no reason she, or anybody else should be attacking anybody with unfounded speculation. If she had been more upset with me than with you, I would probably feel a little differently, but with you being the main person to be attacked..." He trailed off as he got lost in thought. "On the other hand," he looked up at me, the mischievous look back in his eyes, "perhaps finding you a husband would be the best way to dispel the rumors. Is there anybody you have your heart set on already?"

I gaped at him. "I need to get home. Right now. I will see you tomorrow, Pastor Jenkins."

He took a step closer to me as I tried to maneuver around him to leave. "What happened to you calling me Miles?"

"It is too personal of a name, Pastor. If we are to try to keep things more professional, we should call each other by more formal names. Pastor or Pastor Jenkins for you and Miss Stuart for me." I looked him in the eye, daring him to contradict me.

He had a grim look on his face. "I think I know what my sermon will be about next week."

For the second time in as many minutes, my mouth gaped open in astonishment. That had not been the response I was expecting. "What?" I squeaked.

He chuckled. "Judge not, lest ye be judged. Do not spread false rumors. Do not gossip. Etcetera. I think I should be able to tie them all together into one cohesive sermon, don't you?"

I raised an eyebrow and forced my jaw closed. I thought for a minute before nodding. "I'm sure you can. I look forward to hearing how you do it. Until tomorrow, Pastor."

He waved at me as I hurried toward the road home.

CHAPTER ELEVEN

Pastor Jenkins had preached his sermon about gossip, judging others, and spreading rumors. That sermon made him realize how few people actually applied his sermons. Despite the sermon, the rumors about us spread through the town with the speed of a prairie fire. Throughout the next few months, whenever I went to town or to church, instead of people simply not talking to me, they gave me looks of disdain. John noticed it more than I did. The first time I found out that John even saw what they were doing was when his father mentioned it to me.

"John told me people look at you funny when you are in town."

I looked up from the bread I was kneading. "He did?"

Pastor Jenkins nodded. "Is there anything I can do about it?"

I shook my head. "No, nothing will stop them from talking about what they want to talk about. It will eventually die down and life will go back to normal."

He grunted. "I doubt that. John feels bad that people keep looking at you like you are some crook or imposter. I don't know about James because he won't talk about it, but I think he feels even worse."

I brushed some of the flour off my hands and gave Pastor Jenkins my full attention. "If James isn't talking about it, it means that he is hurting inside. I didn't realize it was affecting them so profoundly. I don't mind the looks if they are only affecting me, but those boys, especially James are more sensitive to them." I twisted my hands in my apron and looked down. "And they are rather protective of me."

Pastor Jenkins smiled. "Yes, they are protective of you. You have been the mother figure they needed and they love you very much."

"I'll try not taking them to town as much so they don't see it. Hopefully that will be enough."

Pastor Jenkins shook his head. "No, I don't think that would be a good idea either. If you don't bring them with you, you will be admitting there are things that are beyond God's reach. I will talk to them both tonight. Better yet, I'll talk to them both right now." He turned around and disappeared upstairs.

I stood where I was, stunned and surprised by his reaction. I was still there when all three Jenkins men came down the stairs.

"Are you going to town today, Miss Stuart?" Pastor Jenkins asked.

"Yes, I am."

"Good," he turned to his sons. "Now,

remember what I said and mind what Miss Stuart says."

"Yes, Pa," John answered. I couldn't see either of the boys, but I assumed James either nodded his head or signed a positive response.

Pastor Jenkins turned back to face me. "If they don't behave for you, I want to know as soon as I get home. I'm going to head out and get to work." He walked past me.

"Can I play with my friend William while you do your shopping?" John asked.

"Didn't you get to play with him at school today?"

"Yes, but we didn't finish talking. I wanted to tell him about a dream I had last night. It was the kind of dream you don't wanna tell when others could overhear."

I shook my head and smiled. "Very well, but only for a little while. I'll walk with you to William's house, do my shopping with James, and then come back to William's house."

"Naw, you don't need to do that," John argued. "That would be awful far for you to take all the packages. I'll talk with Will at his house, tell him about the dream, then Will and I can walk to the store." His eyes got wide as an idea came to him. "Can I invite him for supper tonight?"

I cocked an eyebrow. "Well, that would be up to your father and William's parents, but since Pastor Jenkins isn't here, I can't ask him. Let's see what William's mother says."

We walked into town and I let John lead us to William's house. When we got there, John and William disappeared and his mother and I stood in the yard with James and a younger daughter. "John would like to invite William over for dinner tonight. I don't think Pastor Jenkins will have a problem with it if you don't," I started.

"He never has in the past," Mrs. Michaels said with a smile. "I think it is a good idea for them to spend that time together. I know they haven't had much time to be together lately."

I nodded. "I didn't even know John had a friend until today or I would have invited William out to our farm whenever he wanted to join John. As long as he is willing to work, that is."

Mrs. Michaels nodded her head slowly. "That might be a good idea. I'll talk to Zeke about it tonight."

"Well, I should get the shopping done or the boys will be back in town before I get started. It was nice talking to you, Mrs. Michaels."

Mrs. Michaels waved to me as I left. James and I went to the general store and gathered all the things we needed. I ignored the looks and whispers that happened all around me. There may have been only five people in the store, but they still made their presence known in a way that almost made me feel claustrophobic.

Mr. Peterson had just finished wrapping up our last package when John and William came bursting into the store.

"Miss Stuart!" John exclaimed. "You'll never guess what happened."

I spun to face him, a stern look on my face. "John Carlton Jenkins, you know better than to speak in such a loud voice. Go outside and wait for James and me to be finished here. You can tell me what happened when we get back to the house." I turned back to the stunned store owner without waiting to see if John would obey or what his reaction might be. Frankly, I didn't care what his reaction was and I knew he would obey me.

I paid for the items, gave some of the packages to James and picked up the rest. Together, we walked out of the store and walked right past John and William. Making it seem like an afterthought, I turned my head slightly and said, "Come along John and William. Let's get home."

John jogged up to me and tried to take some of the packages out of my arms. "Here, let me help you carry those." I relented and he took half the packages from my arms.

The ten minute walk proceeded in silence. John knew he was in trouble and didn't want to make it worse, and William didn't know what to do with the strict housekeeper. I didn't want to talk right then and James couldn't talk.

When we got to the parsonage, we put the packages on the table and I asked William and James to put the things away while I had a talk with John. They agreed and John and I went to the living room.

"Now, what was it you wanted to tell me?" I asked.

"I wanted to tell you that William can come to supper tonight and that we got to see a foal being born at the stable." John spoke in a subdued voice.

I prayed for wisdom. "That does sound exciting. What did you think?"

John's eyes sparkled when he looked up into my face. I couldn't help letting a smile tug at the corners of my mouth. "I loved it! It was so awe-inspiring to watch a new life be born in the world.

And then only a few minutes after he was born, the foal stood up and started walking around. It was great!"

"I can tell," I said. "Now, what would have been the proper way for you to come into the store to tell me all of this?"

John got a sheepish look on his face. "Go up to you and tell you in a quieter voice or wait until you came out of the store."

I hugged John close to me. "Yes. And knowing you, that is what you will do next time, right?"

John pulled away from my hug. "Yes, Miss Stuart. I will. Will you forgive me for not remembering to keep a quiet voice inside?"

"Yes, John. I forgive you."

John smiled at me. "Thanks."

"Let's go see how William and James are doing."

"Pa? Miss Stuart?" John asked before I left that day. "Can I talk to you, please?"

The two of us exchanged glances and then gave John our full attention.

"What is it, John?" Pastor Jenkins asked.

John took a deep breath and I had a fleeting fear I would not like what he had to say especially since I could tell he was nervous. He was tense and his breathing came in short, raspy breaths.

"Pa, Miss Stuart, I've been thinking for awhile. And praying. I don't know how to say it, or what to say, but Pa, I know you've been trying to match

Miss Stuart up with some of the other men in town because you think she would make a good wife and mother." John glanced over at me and his cheeks turned red as he looked back at his pa. "Well, I've been wondering. Why haven't you ever thought of the possibility of her becoming your wife? I don't want her to get married to someone else. I want her to get married to you so she can be MY ma. James and me need her here. She's been more of a ma to us than anybody I can remember 'cepting ma."

I looked toward James who stood back from our group of three. Tears glistened in his eyes and he signed the words, "I love you, Miss Stuart. I want you as my ma, too."

Tears filled my eyes as I looked over at John and then to Pastor Jenkins. He stood straight and stiff as a board, staring at the far wall.

John took a step toward me and clasped my hand. "Promise me you won't marry anyone besides Pa, Miss Stuart?"

I tried to speak past the knot in my throat, but it took a few tries. I kept my eyes on Pastor Jenkins as I spoke very carefully. "I can't make any promises, John. God might not want your pa and me to get married. He might not ever want me to get married."

"Oh, but He does!" John exclaimed. "He told me you were supposed to be my ma."

That got Miles' attention. He jerked around and stared at his son, eyes wider than Lake Jackson. "How, and when, did He do that?"

"I've been thinking for awhile about this," John said, "and last night when I was praying I really think God agreed with me that Miss Stuart wouldn't marry any of those other men you've been trying to match her with. You're supposed to marry her, Pa. Ain't that right?"

Pastor Jenkins blinked his eyes and took a deep breath. "I...I don't know, John. I'd never really considered it. We don't really know each other..."

"Hogwash," John exclaimed. "Ma was a mail order bride, wasn't she? You two didn't know each other either."

Miles's cheeks turned red. "No, John. That is a story that was spread around. It's not true. Your mother and I practically grew up with each other. The reason folks think she was a mail order bride is because I came here first after getting the job as pastor. I wrote letters to your ma and she wrote back, but we were engaged before I came here." He cleared his throat. "Our original plan was that I would go back there and we would get married, but things got in the way of that and Rebekah decided to come out here to get married."

John shrugged. "Fine. But how much more do you need to know about Miss Stuart? You know she can cook, sew, clean, she's a Christian, you've known each other a little less than a year, and you two get along with each other. What more do you need to know?"

I fought a smile. Ah, the naïveté of a ten year old.

Miles shook his head. "For one thing, she might not want to get married. For another, I would like to know that she at least likes me a little. And there are other things. But, let's get off this subject. It's not one I am ready to talk about right now with you. Besides, Miss Stuart needs to get home now."

I was about to breathe a sigh of relief when John spoke again. "Do you want to get married someday, Miss Stuart?"

My mouth opened, but no words came out at first. I was finally able to stammer, "If God blessed me with a husband, I would marry. But I doubt that will ever happen." I saw Miles's eyes narrow. For some reason, he didn't like it when I said anything about doubting things would happen. I shrugged it off and just about got bowled over with the next question.

"Do you like Pa?" John asked.

"John!" Miles said in a firm, no-nonsense voice. "That is enough. You, William, and James, go into the kitchen and get the table set for supper."

John hung his head and shuffled into the kitchen. James rushed over and gave me a quick hug before following his brother.

"I'm sorry if his questions embarrassed you," Pastor Jenkins said.

"Don't worry about it. I'm a big girl and can handle nosy questions from little boys." I shook my head. "Even if they were misguided questions."

Pastor Jenkins grunted as he held the front door open and stepped onto the porch with me. "Could you stay for a few more minutes? Now is probably the best chance we'll get for awhile to talk about this."

I turned to look at him and he continued on, "It's out in the open right now and very much unresolved. I know I said I didn't want to talk about it, but I mainly didn't want to talk about it in front of the boys. Especially not with William here. I don't know what you're thinking about anything

139

John said and I don't really know what I'm thinking either." He stopped when he looked at me and saw my amused grin. "I'm rambling, aren't I?"

All I could do was nod because I knew I would probably laugh if I opened my mouth.

He took a deep breath. "I'm sorry."

I shook my head. "Don't be. This took us both by surprise." We both stood on the porch, looking and feeling uncomfortable. We looked at everything except each other. There was a peaceful silence for a few minutes. I heard crickets chirping, woodpeckers pecking, birds singing, and squirrels chattering away. I prayed for wisdom and for the words to say while we stood together.

"I feel like I should clarify some of what I said in there," Miles said. "I implied that I would be willing to consider marrying you. I hadn't ever seriously considered it before, not consciously anyway." I heard him swallow hard. "I think we should both pray about it fervently and not take a ten year old's word that God wants us to be married."

I nodded and took a deep breath. "Yes, we do need to pray about it. I love those boys of yours," I said. "Like most girls, I suppose I've always dreamed of marrying a man who I fell madly in love with and who fell madly in love with me. But at my age, you tend to get more realistic about such things. Yes, I do still dream of getting married, and I do still dream of falling in love. However, I think two people can get married and have a form of love based off of friendship and can work on loving each other. Isn't there something in the Bible about loving your enemy? How can you love your enemy if love doesn't take work? The same is true of friends. Even friends will hurt you in some way at some time. But you still need to love them. Love takes work." I laughed a little. "Here I am, standing next to a pastor and giving a little sermon of my own."

I looked over at Pastor Jenkins and saw a grin forming on his face. "Nice sermon. And you thought you could never be a pastor's wife?" We shared a laughing glance. "Well, I'd say we both have some praying to do. If we both agree to explore the possibility of marriage, then I'll have to talk to your pa."

I cringed. "Yes. I suppose you will."

"What is that look for?" Miles asked.

I sighed. "I don't know if Da would allow me to marry anyone, especially not a pastor."

Miles was silent for a long minute. "We'll have to pray that God will soften his heart, if it's meant to be. He's already working on Caleb and I know how much you and the boys have been working on Caleb, too."

"You do?" I asked.

"Sure. Those boys tell me everything." He smiled. "So you better be careful what you say and do around them." He winked at me and I grinned back.

"Well, if we are about done with this conversation, I should really get back home and get supper on the table."

Pastor Jenkins nodded. "I'll see you Friday."

I waved at him as I walked down the porch steps, down the walk and toward home.

During supper, I noticed Caleb staring at me while he chewed on a piece of meat. I cocked my head at him as if to ask, "What is it?" He swallowed his food and mouthed the words, "Let's talk later."

I furrowed my eyebrows and nodded. What would Caleb need to talk to me about? I gave my head a slight shake and went back to eating.

After supper, I washed the dishes while Caleb and Da did the evening chores. Da was the first one inside and he headed straight upstairs. Again. I sighed and prayed that he would someday get over his reclusiveness.

The door creaked open and Caleb came in as I dried the last dish. I looked up at him and noticed his brown hair was getting long again and would need to be cut soon. Caleb took a deep breath and let it all out slowly before collapsing into a chair.

I dried my hands and sat in a chair near him. "What was it you wanted to talk about?"

Caleb stared off into space. "I…John and I've been talking. Da doesn't like it, but we talk when we're working in the fields. You know? He's a really bright boy. And he sure knows his Bible. He's only ten. How does he know these things? Yesterday, when we were taking care of the horses, he asked me about Jed." Caleb stopped talking and I waited for him to go on, but after a minute I realized he wasn't going to.

"What did you say?" I asked.

"Nothin'."

"Nothing? You didn't say anything? Why not?"

Caleb leaned his arms on the table and buried his face in them. "I couldn't," he mumbled.

He kept his head buried for a few minutes. "After I was silent for a couple minutes, he nodded and told me he was that way about his mama for awhile, too. It took a few months before he could talk about her to anyone. Then he told me all about his mama. When he got to the part of her dying, he told me the only thing that made him talk and truly start healing was accepting Christ as his Savior and I should do the same thing."

I raised an eyebrow and Caleb saw it. He gave me a rueful smile. "I didn't respond to that one either and he dropped it. But I've been thinkin' on it all day. I know you've certainly changed and I know it would be good for me, I just don't know that I'm ready for it."

"We can't push you into it either. It has to happen when you are ready. But that won't stop us from praying for you." I made a face as I remembered what else I absolutely had to pray about.

"What's that face for?" Caleb asked.

"Something John said today."

Caleb got a mischievous glitter in his eyes. "Must've been good. What was it?"

I wasn't sure if I was ready to reveal what John had said, but if Miles would be talking to Caleb or Da anytime in the next week or so, I figured I should at least warn Caleb a little. "Well, he said God told him that his da and I should get married and he wants me to be his new ma."

Caleb's eyes went as wide as I had ever seen

them and his jaw just about fell on the floor. "He what? He thinks you should be his ma?"

I shrugged. "Yes."

"Does Miles know about this?"

I nodded.

"What'd he think about it?"

"He wasn't sure what to think. Neither am I. We talked about it a little and agreed to pray about the possibility."

Caleb blinked his eyes rapidly and stared into space. He crossed his arms and leaned on the sideboard, deep in thought. "I guess I assumed you'd be here forever. I know I shouldn't've, but…" He shook his head as if trying to clear a fog from his brain. "I…I'm just shocked is all."

"You're shocked?!?" I asked, incredulous. "What about me and Miles? We had a ten year old practically tell us he thinks God wants me to be his new ma. And all this before Miles and I even dreamt of the possibility of getting married. Yes, we are good friends. But marriage? Me, a pastor's wife?" I took a deep breath to calm myself down. "I'm still a little in shock."

Caleb stood up and came over to me. "I thought you loved those boys."

I looked up at him with a startled gaze. "I do. What made you think otherwise?"

"Well, wouldn't loving the kids be enough?"

I stared at him. "I still have dreams, Caleb. I may be a thirty year old spinster, but I do still have a dream to marry a man I love with all my heart. Maybe it is Miles, maybe it isn't. I don't know. But, God hasn't taken that dream away yet and I'm going to stick with it."

144

Caleb nodded. "I need to get some sleep. It's been a long couple of days."

I nodded and stood up. He headed upstairs and I did a little more cleaning up in the kitchen before going upstairs myself. It took me a long time to actually go to sleep because my mind ran on and on and on about all the events of the day. I was praying about what God wanted for Miles and me when I finally fell into a deep, dreamless sleep.

CHAPTER TWELVE

Sunday dawned bright and clear. I got into my Sunday dress and headed down to the kitchen. As we ate breakfast, I was surprised to see Caleb ate his breakfast in more of a hurry than usual. I was about to question him when he excused himself from the table and strode up the stairs, taking the steps two at a time. Da and I exchanged a puzzled glance, but neither of us knew what was going on.

Da had gone out to the barn and I had dried and put away the last breakfast dish when Caleb walked down the stairs. I turned to ask him what in the world he was doing, but the words died when they reached the tip of my tongue. I stared at him. He was dressed in a broadcloth suit I hadn't known existed. It looked professionally tailored and was a perfect fit for him. I had never seen him in such a nice outfit and I admit I had to look him over from head to toe.

When my eyes returned to his face, I noticed the embarrassed and sheepish look he wore.

"What's the occasion?" I asked. "Funeral? Wedding?" I wiggled my eyebrows and grinned mischievously. "A girl catch your eye?"

Caleb actually blushed. If I hadn't seen it with my own eyes, I wouldn't have believed it possible.

He cleared his throat. "No, ma'am. I decided it was high time you have a male escort to church. Especially now that Miles has expressed his intention to court you."

"He has?" I asked. I tried to recall what had happened the last two days and when Miles and Caleb could have spoken to each other. Nothing came to mind.

"Yep. I was supposed to tell you yesterday, but chose to wait 'til today. I hope you don't mind that I waited."

"I'm glad you did. I wouldn't have slept a wink if you had told me last night. But when did you and Miles talk?"

"Just before he came to get the boys. Da and I were out in the field near the road and Miles stopped to help us and talk. Da and I had been struggling to put two fence rails back in place and Miles came by in time to help us. Da's ribs were bothering him again and Da was appreciative and impressed that he would take the time to help us and that he knew exactly what to do."

I cocked an eyebrow. "I imagine so."

Caleb nodded. "When we were finished, he talked to us and Da and I both gave him permission to court you. As I'm sure you know, Da doesn't want to be involved at all. He thinks you're old enough to make your own decisions without needing him to be there all the time."

I pulled on the apron strings and lifted the apron over my head. "Yes, but the accountability…"

"Miles has asked me to be that person for you. He said we've got a close enough relationship and you would probably confide in me about almost anything." Caleb shrugged.

I looked up at him and nodded. "That is good. Yes, I think that will work. Does Miles have someone he can confide in?"

Caleb held out his arm to me and I put my elbow in the crook of his arm as we headed for the door. I grabbed Mama's Bible as we walked past the table.

"He said he had a couple of people in mind and would be speaking to them today."

We walked to the road in silence. As he turned toward town, I had a sudden thought. "Does Da know you are coming with me?"

Caleb stiffened slightly. "No."

I nodded, deep in thought. I chose not to consider what Da would think. I knew he would be upset that both of his children were going to church, but I also knew church was more important and maybe, just maybe, Da would start thinking about God in a good way.

It didn't seem to take quite as long to get to church. As we walked into the church yard, I felt many eyes turn our direction. Were they looking to see who was with me or were they simply staring at the handsome brother escorting me? I didn't have time to wonder about it long since two boys barreled toward us.

"You came! You came!" John shouted as he neared us.

Caleb let go of me and took one long step

toward John, grabbed his arms, and swung him around. "Yes, sir, I did. When I promise somethin', I do it." Caleb looked over at me and gave me a wink.

James snuggled up next to me and I gave him a small squeeze. "How are you today, James?"

"Fine," he signed.

I smiled at him and looked back toward John and Caleb. I almost had to force myself not to scan the church yard for Miles. He was probably in the church anyway and not outside. I gave myself a mental shake and felt James tugging at me to leave the chattering John with Caleb.

We weaved our way through the yard, holding hands and enjoying each others' company. We had gotten about halfway through the yard when I saw a group of young women heading the opposite direction, their eyes set on a point behind us. I looked over my shoulder in the general direction they were headed and saw only Caleb.

I stopped suddenly as I realized what was happening. Caleb was a handsome, eligible young man. I'd never really thought about it before, but he was probably one of the most handsome young men in town. And he was new to church. Out of the corner of my eye, I saw James looking at me with confusion in his eyes. *After church should be interesting,* I thought. In the same instant I had a sudden fear as to how Caleb would take all the attention. I tried to shrug off the fear as not being my problem, but if it kept Caleb from coming back to church... *God,* I prayed silently, *help Caleb, please.*

150

We didn't even get out of church before the young ladies swarmed around us again. Or rather, Caleb. I barely sneaked past before getting smothered and forgotten. As I shook Miles' hand, Miles whispered, "Can we talk after the rest of the congregation has gone?"

I nodded. "As long as Caleb doesn't mind waiting."

Miles smiled and turned to the person behind me. I walked out of the church and took a deep breath. August definitely wasn't my favorite month of the year, but it did help the garden grow and ripen.

I looked around the yard and saw that most people were already on their way home. It was a hot day and I think they wanted to get into the shade of their houses. I stood next to the church building to stay out of the sun. I was there only a few minutes before the gaggle of girls traipsed out of the church followed closely by Caleb and Miles.

The two men talked as they walked down the steps. Caleb gave Miles a nod and went over to where John and James were playing with a couple of other boys.

As I watched Caleb join the boys in whatever it was they were playing, Miles approached me.

"Are you ready to talk?"

I swallowed. "I think so. Although, I'm not sure what you want to talk about."

Miles looked down at his hands and was quiet for a long time. "I'm really not sure how to do this courting thing with you," he admitted. "It's been a long while since I courted a girl and then it was with someone I knew growing up. This just seems so different." He looked over at me, pain evident in his eyes. "I have to be honest, I loved my wife and I'm not sure...I don't know if I could love someone else. I," his voice faltered, "I don't know."

Hoping he wouldn't think me too forward, I put a hand on his arm. "I understand."

Miles forced a smile. "Thank you. You know, it's been awhile since I've had someone I felt like I could confide in. It's going to take a lot of adjustment."

"It'll be harder for me," I said. "I've never had someone like that. Caleb a little, but even with him, I don't. I'll be learning from scratch."

"Knowing you, Anna, you will learn quickly and learn well."

I turned my face away from him to hide the tears that sprang to my eyes. "Thank you."

"Well, I suppose I should let you go now," Miles said. "It looks like Caleb is ready to go."

I glanced over to where Caleb stood near the boys. "Yes, I believe you are correct."

Caleb saw us looking at him and walked over. "You ready?"

I put my hand on his arm. "Yes, I am."

Caleb nodded to Miles. "Good to see you again, Miles."

"Same to you, Caleb. I look forward to seeing you on Tuesday and next Sunday."

"Don't push your luck, Preacher," Caleb said with a smile.

"I don't believe in luck," Miles answered. "I

believe in prayer."

Caleb cocked an eyebrow, but didn't respond.

"I'll see you three tomorrow," I said.

"Bye, Miss Stuart!" John replied.

Caleb and I walked slowly home, neither of us wanting to face Da. Our fears were unfounded since when we arrived home, Da wasn't even around. Caleb searched for him and found him passed out in the barn, so we ate our lunch without him.

A few weeks later, Caleb was still accompanying me to church. It was almost exactly one year since we had received the letter from Jed, and I had started to get a little depressed. The courtship had gone well thus far and Miles and I spent as much time as we dared after he came home and before I left.

The Sunday of my first anniversary of attending church, Miles preached an excellent sermon about humility. I couldn't wait to hear what Caleb had to say about it. We didn't even get out of church before the young ladies swarmed around us again. Or rather, Caleb. I barely sneaked past before getting smothered and forgotten. As I shook Miles' hand, I whispered to him, "Good luck getting those girls to leave Caleb alone long enough to shake your hand." I gave a nod toward the group.

Miles took a look behind me and grinned. "Better him than me," he said.

I laughed and headed outside. I took a deep breath and breathed in the cool, refreshing air. As I stepped off the bottom stair, a hand darted for my arm and I automatically flinched away from it.

"Don't you dare try to run away from me, young lady," a sharp voice snapped.

I turned toward the voice and saw Mrs. Morgan glaring at me. "I wasn't aware that I was running away."

"Perhaps you weren't, but you should be," Mrs. Morgan said.

I looked at her in confusion. "Is there something wrong?"

"Of course there is. It's rumored all around town that you and Pastor Jenkins are going to get married."

"What?" I choked. "We haven't talked…"

"Pish posh." She waved my words off. "I heard John talking about you courting. Don't think you can hide that from us."

I stood up as tall as I could and looked at her with narrowed eyes. "And what exactly is the problem with Pastor Jenkins and me courting?"

Mrs. Morgan looked up at me with disdain. "You are the problem. Until almost a year ago, you were a hermit. You rarely came to town and when you did, it wasn't to be friendly or to make friends. In fact, you seemed to shun everybody who tried to be friendly with you. Now, you are suddenly coming to church and making friends with everybody: John, James, Pastor Jenkins, that negro woman, the new woman Wilma, and who knows who else." She stopped to catch her breath. "As far as I can tell, you aren't a real Christian and you are going to corrupt all these good people who are and have gone to church their whole lives." As she finished, the look in her eyes changed from disdain to a challenge.

My quick temper flared up briefly as I stood there, dumbfounded and speechless. I had no argument to defend myself with. Anything I said for myself would be considered prideful and would be counterproductive. As my brain processed this information, a young voice piped into the conversation and I became aware of the crowd of people near us.

"Begging your pardon, Mrs. Morgan, but Miss Stuart is a Christian. She has been for a year now. She is friends with people now because Jesus changed her heart and mind. I think she's always been friendly, but she hid it for awhile because she didn't feel worthy of having friends and no one was friendly to her." John's eyes blazed with righteous anger. "And she most definitely ain...isn't corrupting anybody. If anything, she's helped James and me get more uncorrupt than before by encouraging us in productive things instead of what we were doing before."

John gave me a quick glance and I tried to smile at him. "Pa's said a few times now that he's learned things from her that helped him, too. I don't know about the butcher's wife or Mrs. Wilma, but have you seen any supposed-to-be Christians talking to either of them much? I know I haven't. And why not? Just because the butcher married a negro woman? And just because Mrs. Wilma's new, don't mean she can't be associated with. Miss Stuart's acted more like a Christian these last couple of months than I've seen any of you do in the last couple of years." When he was finished, he spread his legs apart and crossed his arms across his chest, defying anybody to refute what he said.

Mrs. Morgan stared at John as did I. As we stared at the ten year old philosopher, someone started clapping. I looked up and the crowd had grown bigger.

Someone in the middle of the group shouted, "Who thinks this young man'll be our next preacher?"

A nervous laugh rippled through the crowd and the tension between Mrs. Morgan and I dissipated.

"All right people. Show's over. Let's get moving," Miles announced from the top of the stairs. "I think we all have better things to do than stand around gawking at my son." He lowered his voice as he came down the stairs and stood next to Mrs. Morgan. "John, I'll be talking to you later. Mrs. Morgan, next time you want to make accusations about someone, I suggest you think them through first.

"And while you're thinking about them, remember Matthew 7:1-5: 'Judge not, that you be not judged. For with the judgment you pronounce you will be judged, and with the measure you use it will be measured to you. Why do you see the speck that is in your brother's eye, but do not notice the log that is in your own eye? Or how can you say to your brother, "Let me take the speck out of your eye," when there is the log in your own eye? You hypocrite, first take the log out of your own eye, and then you will see clearly to take the speck out of your brother's eye.'"

I smiled as I started to walk away. As I was about to take my first step, a gentle hand rested on my shoulder. Since the crowd had dispersed already, I wondered who it could be. I turned my head and saw Miles looking at me. I turned back to look at him fully and raised a questioning eyebrow.

"I wanted to tell you everything John said was true. I'm proud of the woman you have become. From what I've heard from the talk of those who grew up with you, you seem to be acting more like you did when you were younger."

"What do you mean by that?" I asked.

"Meaning before your mother died and you were forced to take all the responsibility of Jed and the house on your shoulders."

"I wasn't forced to do that," I interrupted. "I begged Da to let me take care of Jed. I didn't want Jed to leave, too. Not right after Mama died. I was afraid if Da sent him away, we'd never get him back."

Miles looked at me with a look I couldn't figure out in his eyes. "You begged your father to let you do that? You wanted to have the responsibility?"

I nodded. "Yes, I did. Da was going to send Jed away to someone who could feed him. We had a cow, so I told Da I could do it. I was nine and had been doin' all the cooking and cleaning practically since Mama found out she was pregnant. She was really sick through the whole thing." I looked off into the distance past Miles' head. "That was the hardest year and a half of my life. I was a mother at the age of nine. I did all the cooking, cleaning, and feeding. Plus trying to keep up with my school work."

Miles shook his head in amazement. "I always knew you were an amazing woman, but now I know better. You are more than just an amazing woman; you are an incredibly talented and blessed woman."

Warmth rose to my cheeks and I ducked my head in embarrassment. "Thank you."

Miles nodded and looked around the nearly empty yard. "I think your brother is waiting for you. I'm glad he came."

I followed his gaze to where Caleb stood by himself, near us, but not too close. "I am, too. I wonder where all his admirers went."

Caleb must have seen us looking toward him and decided to come over. He heard my last comment, too.

"Ah, I just said somethin' and they all made excuses to leave."

I puzzled over what he could have said to scare them off, but decided to ask on the way home. I looked around for John and James. "I'll see you three tomorrow," I said when I spotted them nearby.

John grinned. "I can't wait."

"Why?" I asked, instantly curious.

"Because," he answered mysteriously.

I glanced at James and he signed the words, "It's a secret."

I shook my head in amusement. "Okay, okay, I'll try to wait until tomorrow.

"You ready to go home?" Caleb asked.

I nodded, noticing the haunted look in his eyes. From long experience, I knew better than to push Caleb into conversation about anything very serious. Instead, I decided to ask him just one question and then let him lead the conversation. "What did you say to those girls to make them scatter?"

Caleb chuckled and started toward home. "I asked if any of them were over twenty three or had kids."

"What? Why did you ask that?"

Caleb put his arm in mine and said, "I'm partial to older women who are either widows or at least almost out of their twenties. None of them were or were willing to admit it, so they left."

"Why those particular facts?" I asked.

"I'm getting old, Anna. I'm thirty-two, work long hours in the fields, I hardly say a hundred words a day, even to you. I'm far from being a poet and I'm not all that good with kids. I've made some bad decisions in my life, and I'm not a devout Christian like you and don't see myself ever becoming one."

I was quiet for a few minutes while we walked down the tree-lined roads. "If any woman thinks you would've never made a bad decision in your life, she'd better rethink her priorities. As for you becoming a Christian, you never know what God's plan is. He could win you over yet," I said with a grin.

Caleb and I walked on in silence until we reached the edge of our property. "What about my age?"

"Caleb Iain Stuart! You are only thirty-two. That is the prime of life, not old age. Sure, some men marry at the age of eighteen, but not all. If you're too old, the girl's father won't allow you to court her. Don't worry about such silly nonsense."

Caleb stepped back and held his hands up in surrender. "Yes, ma'am. I think I get the picture." He sighed and mumbled something under his breath.

I narrowed my eyes at him. "Is there a woman in particular you are worried will think you are too old?"

Two mottled, red spots showed up on Caleb's cheeks. "Who said there was someone?"

I bit my lip in an attempt to keep from smiling. "Well, you kind of implied it."

Caleb grunted. "It's nothing."

I grabbed Caleb's arm as he tried to get away from me. "Caleb, there is no need to be embarrassed. You have every right to like a woman. I…" I swallowed hard. "Just like I have every right to like a man." My cheeks suddenly grew hot.

Caleb turned on me and we stood in the middle of the road, staring at each other. "Do you? Like a man, I mean?"

I laughed and wagged a finger at him. "I asked first, Brother. You have to answer before I think about answering."

Caleb grimaced. "Shucks, I was hoping to trick you into saying you like Miles." He started walking along the road again. After a few more yards, he spoke up. "Her name is Maggie."

I searched my memory, but couldn't remember anybody I knew named Maggie. "Who's Maggie?"

Caleb cleared his throat a few times. "She's a woman I've been writing to. I've never actually met her in person."

"And?" I prompted when he was silent too long.

"And what?"

"How did you find her?"

160

"I saw an ad in the paper. She was advertising to become a mail order bride. I wrote her and we've written a few times. She's also writing another guy, but her last letter said he found someone else and she wants to come meet me. She wants to stay at the boarding house for a little while to let us get to know each other in person before deciding if we wanna marry. I'm not sure yet what to think."

I listened in stunned silence. When he finished, I blurted out the first question that came to mind. "How old is she?"

"She's thirty-one and has a daughter from her first marriage. I should've probably told you that. Her husband died two years ago and she's starting to run out of money and no one will hire her. Her daughter's name is Rachel and she's ten."

"So what happened to all your worries about the young women?"

Caleb scuffed his toe in the dirt as we stopped outside our front yard. "They're still there. I'm afraid when she sees me, she'll see who I really am and won't like me. I'm worried she'll see how hard it is to work the farm and what long hours I have to work. It's unfair to her daughter that I'm no good with kids. Even if we don't have any of our own, Rachel'll still need a father. Maggie's a devout Christian, too. What if she rejects me because I'm not a Christian?" He cleared his throat as if uncomfortable. "There's other things, too."

I stepped in front of Caleb and put my hand on his chin, forcing him to look at me. "Caleb, these are all things you will have to work out on your own and with Maggie. If it is God's will for you to marry Maggie, He will work it out. Even if that means you becoming a Christian. As for you not being good with children, that's hogwash and you know it. You've done great with the Jenkins boys when they're here."

"Yeah, but they're boys."

"So what?" I protested. "I still think you'll be good with children, girls or boys. Just watch, if Maggie comes here, Rachel'll be glued to your side the entire time."

Caleb shrugged. "Now you have to answer my question." His grin turned mischievous and I groaned.

"Do I have to?" I asked.

"Yes," he said, holding my arm captive while I tried to walk away.

"Miles," I said.

"Really? I know you two are courting, but I thought it was more for John and James."

"No. And don't you dare tell him, John, or James, either!" I commanded.

Caleb chuckled. "Yes'm. Wouldn't the gossips love to hear that?"

I glared at him and he let go of me and backed away. "Sorry, I didn't mean anything by it," he apologized. "I wouldn't say anything to them either. I'd rather just tell Miles. But I'll keep it to myself if you keep quiet about Maggie and Rachel."

I nodded. "I will."

"Now we'd best get inside before Da thinks we're lazy bums."

Caleb opened the door and I stepped through with Caleb following close behind.

"Where do you think you went, Caleb Stuart?" Da demanded as we walked in.

Da stood in the kitchen doorway, bottle in hand, eyes bleary with drink and pain.

Caleb stood up straight. "I went to church again with Anna."

"Yer not gonna be one of them lily-livered Christians are ye?" Da asked.

"I don't know yet," Caleb responded. "If I am, I won't be a lily-livered one at the very least."

I stayed behind Caleb hoping Da wouldn't see me, but he did. Da snorted at Caleb's answer and glared at me. "Ye'd better not go corruptin' me boy, Anna Stuart. If ye do, ye'll be kicked outta this house before ye can wonder what be goin' on."

"I'll not be corrupting Caleb, Da. If he becomes a genuine Christian, I lay no claims to it. God's the only one who can do that. And I wouldn't call it being corrupted, either."

"And," Caleb interrupted me, "I chose to go of my own free will. Anna was as surprised that I was going as anybody else. Well, except John, who practically begged me to come."

Da stared at Caleb. His voice was gruff and full of conviction when he next spoke. "What you two need to do is get married and get outta me house."

My mouth dropped open. "What?" I squeaked.

"Ye heard me, Anna," Da said. "I wanna be able to live here by meself."

"You've never told us that before," Caleb said. From the look on his face, he was as confused as I was.

"That's because I knew it wouldn't do any good. Now with Anna being courted by that Pastor," he nearly spat the last word out, "at least one o' ye

163

seems to be doin' something."

Caleb and I exchanged a glance. "We don't always tell you everything," Caleb said in a quiet voice.

Da glanced between the two of us sharply. "What're ye saying? Ye are doing somethin', Caleb?"

"They're still figuring things out," I said. "But, Da, I thought Caleb would be living here with you."

"He can build a cabin o' his own somewhere on me land and we'll still farm together. But, nay, he'll not be livin' with me once he's married. If he ever is." At that, Da turned and went back into the kitchen.

"It should be an interesting couple of months," Caleb said. "Maybe I'll write to Maggie tomorrow and ask her and Rachel to come out in about four months or so. That should give me enough time to at least get started on a house."

"Talk to Miles. You and him could organize a house raising."

Caleb stared at me. "They would do that?"

"They would love to help you out, Caleb."

"But I'm practically a stranger to them!" Caleb protested.

"That doesn't matter. If someone in the community needs help they rally around that person."

"Unless it's their own pastor," Caleb commented.

"They rallied around him for awhile, but after a year or so, they thought he could handle it on his own. And he could have if he'd been a farmer or store owner. But pastors and doctors both have so

164

many more responsibilities and they need to be on call at all hours of the day and night."

"Could you mention it to Miles tomorrow?" Caleb asked.

"I'll have to tell him about Maggie and Rachel."

Caleb looked away. "Whatever you need to do."

"Sure, I can do that. Should I also mention he should start courting me fast in case I get kicked out when you become a Christian?"

"WHEN I become a Christian?" Caleb raised his right eyebrow. "You don't know everything I've done. God wouldn't let me in heaven and I don't want to talk about it."

I cocked my head and looked at him.

"I still think God can do a miracle with you, Caleb."

"Aren't you puttin' the cart before the horse there, Anna?"

I laughed. "Nah, it's called woman's intuition." I sidled a glance at him. "Or wishful thinking."

Caleb threw his head back in laughter as he moved past me to go upstairs and change.

CHAPTER THIRTEEN

Monday morning dawned clear and bright, but John missed the sunrise. An hour before, he had gotten up and awakened James and the two had been scurrying here and there and everywhere else since.

James lay on the floor in the entryway, tongue hanging out, in deep concentration. His hands were fisted around a small paintbrush as he worked with painstaking care on a large piece of paper.

Meanwhile, John was hard at work in the kitchen, his father supervising a baking operation from the table, a Bible open in front of him and a pad of paper under his right hand, a stub of pencil poised in his fingers.

There was flour on John's right cheek, on the tip of his nose, and all over the large apron. He sighed heavily and held a bowl of batter in his arms as he walked toward his father. "Does this look about right, Pa?" he asked.

Miles looked up from his Bible and notes and

into the bowl. John gave it a quick stir. Miles pondered the question. "Yes, I think it does look good. I guess we will find out when we eat it."

John nodded with a solemn look on his face as he walked back to the counter and poured the batter into a pan. "You think her pa will come tonight?"

Miles chuckled. "I doubt it, but he might surprise us."

"I hope so. I think that would be the best surprise of the day for Miss Stuart." He finished dumping the batter into the pan and put the bowl in the sink before looking at the recipe. "Pa, could you put it in the oven for me?"

Miles stood up and walked over to his son. "Of course."

While Miles put the cake in the oven, John took the warm water off the stove and dumped it and some soap into the bowl in the sink and started washing the dishes. "When are you and Miss Stuart going to get married, Pa?"

Miles looked up from his notes. "What?"

"When're you and Miss Stuart going to get married?"

Miles sighed as he realized he wasn't going to get much work done this morning. "We've courted for almost two months. I know it seems simple to you, but marriage is for life and if you are going to spend the rest of your life with someone, you want to make sure it is the right person. It will probably take Miss Stuart and me at least a few months to decide if we want to get married."

"So you might get married before Christmas?"

Miles did some quick math. Christmas was

only a few months away. "I doubt it. Maybe sometime after the start of the next year or maybe even as late as next spring." He held up a hand to interrupt John before he protested. "One of the fruits of the Spirit is patience. Now would be a good time to start cultivating that fruit."

John ducked his head and returned to the dishes. "Yes, Pa."

James walked in with a huge grin on his face.

"Finished, James?" Miles asked.

A vigorous nod from James got John's spirits back up.

"Let's go see it, Pa!" John grabbed a semi-dry towel and wiped his hands on it before taking a couple of quick steps toward the other room.

Miles glanced at the clock as he walked past. "We'd better get the sign hung soon or Anna will get here before we're finished."

John changed direction and ran outside to get the hammer and nails out of the tool shed while James and Miles brought two chairs from the kitchen into the entryway.

When John returned, he handed the hammer and nails to his father and clambered onto the opposite chair. James handed them the sign and John held his side up while Miles hammered his side into the wood. When that was done, he stepped off the chair and moved over to where John stood on his tiptoes. Miles took hold of the sign and motioned for John to get down. John jumped off and stood back.

"How's it look, boys?" Miles asked.

James motioned his hand upward and Miles moved it up a couple inches.

"Down a little more," John said. Miles moved

it down bit by bit, his head turned toward his sons, watching for a nod. After about half an inch, John looked over at James who studied the sign with miniscule care before bobbing his head in a down-up motion. Miles pounded the last nail in and then stood back to admire the sign.

"Wonderfully done, James," he said. "You have always amazed me with your artistic abilities."

John grinned and slapped his brother on the back. "Great job, James. Now to go see if my masterpiece turned out nearly as good as James' did." John raced into the kitchen.

"Pa!" He shouted. "It looks perfect! Can you check to see if it is done baking, please?"

Miles shook his head. This was why he had an office at the church. He would never get a sermon done here. He walked into the kitchen and opened the oven. One glance told him it wasn't even close to ready yet.

"Not yet. Go finish washing the dishes and cleaning up the house, then I'll check on it again."

While the boys scurried around picking up every stray piece of anything, Miles sat at the table trying to concentrate on his sermon. Half an hour and two sentences later, he heaved a sigh and gave up.

Knowing John would be in the kitchen soon, Miles got up and checked the cake. He tapped the top of the cake lightly with his fingertips and gave a shrug as John walked into the kitchen "I think it's done." He carefully lifted the confection out of the oven and set it on the table. "There. Now it just needs to cool. And it is time for you two to get ready for school. I'll try to delay Anna when she gets here." As the boys ran to their room, he muttered, "If I can."

John and James scurried about the house gathering and packing what they needed for school while Miles stepped outside onto the porch to wait for Anna.

Miles was surprised to feel so nervous and excited about the surprise his sons had planned with Caleb's help. When he saw movement in the corner of his eye, his breath caught and his muscles grew tense. He hadn't felt this nervous about something since he preached his first sermon over eleven years before. Why should he be so nervous about this? It was Caleb and his sons who had planned everything, not him. He took a deep breath and stepped off the porch as Anna drew near.

"Good morning, Anna," he said.

She had a confused look on her face. "Good morning, Miles. Why the welcoming committee?"

"John and James are finishing up the surprise they have for you."

Anna's laugh filled the small yard. "You know, I still have absolutely no idea what they are up to."

"Ah, but I do, so you should be able to trust that they aren't getting into too much trouble," Miles teased.

Anna raised an eyebrow. "Sometimes I wonder if you aren't more of a troublemaker than they are."

Miles chuckled. "Bekah would have said the same thing." He was about to continue when the door behind them flew open and a breathless John burst outside, his shirt half tucked in and his hair flying in every direction.

"She can come in now. Hi, Miss Stuart."

"Hello, John," Anna said with a smile.

John hopped down the steps and grabbed her

171

hand. "Come on, you've gotta see what we did."

Anna allowed herself to be pulled inside. John stopped inside the door and Anna's eyes went right to the sign that read, "Happy Birthday, Miss Stuart!" in large, childish block letters. Surrounding the words was a beautiful, well organized design of swirls and flowers.

Anna turned toward where James stood away from the group at the doorway. Tears were in her eyes as she took a step towards him. "James, did you do that?"

James nodded.

"It's beautiful. Thank you." She knelt down and held out her arms. James ran into them and they hugged until John tugged on her sleeve.

"There's more, Miss Stuart."

Anna stood up and avoided Miles' gaze as the tears continued to cloud her eyes. As John led her into the kitchen, she tried to stem the flow.

"Look what I made!" John exclaimed.

Anna looked in the direction John pointed. "You made me a cake?" Anna asked, incredulity seeping out of her voice.

John nodded his head vigorously.

Anna stepped around the table to get a closer look at the cake. It wasn't perfect, but it was chocolate and it smelled good. She felt John to her right, put her arm around his shoulders, and gave him a quick hug. "Thank you, John. Nobody has ever made me a birthday cake before."

She turned around to face Miles. "How did any of you know today was my birthday?"

Miles' eyes twinkled. "That is for us to know and you not to find out."

"Caleb told somebody, didn't he?" Anna asked,

172

looking each of them in the eyes as she asked. Miles and John both kept straight faces, but James grinned and nodded.

Anna laughed. "I knew I could count on you, James." She glanced up at the clock. "But, it is time for two young boys to get off to school and one old boy to get off to work."

A collective groan sounded through the room.

"What's this? I thought as Birthday Girl, you three were supposed to do whatever I said without complaint." Anna cocked an eyebrow, fighting a losing battle at keeping the smile off her face as she made up a new rule for her birthday.

"Yes, ma'am," John said, in a disappointed tone. James and John picked up their lunch boxes and school books and Miles and Anna walked with them to the door.

"Have a good day at school, boys. I'll have the cake ready for your after school snack."

John's face instantly brightened. "Yippee!!" He ran down to the road and James followed suit.

Miles turned to Anna. "You sure know how to make their day, don't you?"

Anna looked up at him and smiled. "I try to anyway."

Miles laughed. When he turned his twinkling eyes back toward Anna, he gave her an impish grin. "If I come home after school is out, can I get a piece of cake, too, Miss Stuart?" His twinkling eyes turned into begging puppy eyes.

Anna chuckled. "I'll consider it."

Miles gave a dramatic sigh and slowly turned to leave. "Okay, see ya later."

Anna gave a quick wave before turning back to the house and getting to work on the cleaning.

CHAPTER FOURTEEN

I was surprised by how clean the kitchen was considering it was John who had baked the cake. He had even washed the dishes he had dirtied. One thing I had noticed in the few months that I had known the Jenkins' was that John was the carefree, careless one; James was careful, clean, and meticulous, almost obsessively so. And then there was Miles. Miles was carefree, but mostly clean and careful. Some days, his belongings would be put away and other days, they would be strewn everywhere. It was almost as if he were two different people warring with each other.

Lord, help Miles. He seems so calm and carefree today, but somehow I also feel he is hiding something deep down. Help him to release his pain, or whatever it is, to You, Lord. And if he needs someone to talk to, help him to find that person and help them to be willing and open to listening.

After getting water heated while I cleaned up what John had missed, I did my usual Monday laundry and hung it out to dry. By the time that was finished, it was lunchtime and I fixed myself a little something to eat. I was about to start making supper when the front door opened. I smoothed the apron on my skirt while I went to see who was walking in.

"Miles? What is it?"

Miles looked chagrined. "I forgot to tell you not to make supper tonight. Caleb and I are treating you and the boys at the restaurant."

"And Da?" I asked, expecting a negative answer, but still hoping I was wrong.

"Caleb said he would try." Miles looked at the floor and his arms hung helplessly at his sides.

I nodded, disappointment flooding through me.

"Thank you," I whispered. I turned back to the kitchen before he could see the tears stinging my eyes.

"Anna," Miles' voice stopped me short. It was filled with sorrow and longing, but longing for what?

I tried to swallow the lump in my throat. "Yes?"

"I wish I could've told you differently. I want your da there, too." He took a deep breath and whispered, "I cannot imagine what it must have been like for you growing up."

I held my back rigidly straight and struggled for breath as the tears rolled down my cheeks. I felt more than heard Miles take two quick steps toward me. A hand tentatively touched my shoulder and gently caressed it.

It took me a full minute to stop my tears and control my breathing. Once the tears were gone, I wiped my eyes hurriedly and turned to Miles.

Eyes downcast, I said, "Thank you for letting me know about dinner." I swallowed hard again.

Miles put a finger under my chin and lifted it up. "You're welcome, Anna. I will pray all afternoon that your father will come tonight."

I pursed my lips, to keep my lower lip from trembling. "Thank you," I whispered.

Miles looked into my face intently for a few seconds and then turned around abruptly and left the house. As soon as he was gone, I hid my face in the apron and wept. *Oh God, why does it have to be so hard? Why does Da always have to ruin things for me? Why couldn't he show just one small little ounce of love for me? All I ever asked for was a small bit of caring from him. A hug once in awhile, a gentle word, or a smile would've done it. Why, God, why?*

I don't know how long I stood there crying into my apron, but when I was done, I hung it out to dry since I had thoroughly soaked it. I then splashed cold water on my face to get rid of most of the evidence of my weeping and took a deep breath to calm my shattered nerves. At least I didn't have to worry about supper. Now all I had to do was frost the cake.

Three boys showed up for afternoon snack. One of them was a bit overgrown, but he sure acted like a boy, except for the concerned look he gave me when he walked in the door behind his sons. Their excitement helped lift my mood.

"You okay now?" he whispered as he walked passed me.

I nodded and gave a half grin. "I'm fine."

His eyes searched mine and seemed to see the

half-truth I had just told, but he didn't say anything about it.

Once the cake was cut and dished up, we all sat there and stared at John.

"What?" he asked.

"We're waiting for you to take the first bite, Son," Miles said with a grin.

"Oh. Okay." He cut a large bite and stabbed it with his fork. We all watched as the piece of cake disappeared into his mouth and he started chewing. "Mmm," he said. "This is good. If I do say so myself." He winked at us.

We all laughed and dug in. The cake really was good. I could hardly believe a ten year old had made it. "You should start a bakery, John," I said.

John's eyes grew wide as saucers. "No way, no ma'am. I ain't doin' that!"

"Why not?" I asked, choosing to ignore his grammar.

John shook his head. "I'd never have the patience to do it."

Miles chuckled. "Plus, I think he's rather young to start a business."

The conversation ended there and as soon as we were finished with our cake, we all went our separate ways. Miles went back to the church to put some finishing touches on whatever he was doing there, John and James got their homework finished, and I went home to get ready for my first meal at the hotel restaurant.

As I walked home, I wondered if Caleb had told Miles I had never been to a restaurant or that it was my thirtieth birthday. I shook my head. Probably not. Those weren't things a man would likely think of, especially Caleb. Then again, planning a surprise birthday party wasn't exactly something I would have expected him to think of either.

When I got home and went up to my room, I stared at the dresses hanging in my wardrobe. Which dress should I wear? One of my less-worn work dresses or my church dress? I pulled two dresses out of my wardrobe and laid them on the bed. My church dress had a dark green background with light green leaf filigree weaving through the fabric. The other dress I had pulled out was my nicest work dress. It was made of a heavier material and was a plain mauve color with maroon trim around the waist, hem, and the bottoms of the sleeves.

"How about instead of wearing one of those old things, you wear this one?"

I jumped at the sound of Caleb's voice and stared at him with wide eyes. He held a dress made from the material I had always wanted a dress made from. It was a light blue with dark blue roses scattered around the material. There was dark blue trim around the collar, hem, and sleeve hems. At the waist, the trim bordered a flowery lace.

My breath caught in my throat as my hand went up to the same spot. "Where in the world…?" I couldn't finish the sentence.

Caleb gave me a sheepish look and a slight shrug. "I saw you fingering this material a few months ago. When I started plannin' this surprise birthday for you, I decided to ask Wilma to make you a dress. I told her what material to use and I paid her to make it for you."

Tears ran down my cheeks for the second time that day. This time, they were tears of joy rather than pain. "Oh, Caleb, thank you!" I ran to him and gave him a hug and kissed him on the cheek. "Thank you so much. I can't believe you did this for me."

Caleb cleared his throat in embarrassment and shrugged his shoulders. "It wasn't all that much."

I took the dress from him and said, "It was much more than you will ever know, Caleb. Now get out of here so I can try this on and make sure I don't need to make any last minute adjustments to it."

Caleb gave me a half grin and a mock salute. "Yes'm, Miss Stuart."

The dress fit perfectly. I had no idea how Wilma did it without knowing my measurements, but she somehow guessed exactly right. When I came downstairs half an hour later, after arranging my hair in a less severe manner, I found Caleb and Da both waiting for me in the kitchen. Da stared at me in shock and amazement.

Caleb's eyes went wide, but he at last found his voice. "Good evening, Miss Stuart," he teased. "I can't wait to see Miles' reaction when he sees you dressed like this."

I blushed and swatted Caleb's arm. "Hush, Caleb!"

I turned to Da and was surprised to see he had on a clean shirt and his nicest pair of pants.

I froze. "Da, are you coming with us?"

Da cleared his throat. "Aye, Caleb convinced me 'twas only right to come along."

I barely managed to curb my impulse to hug him. "Thank you, Da."

"Shall we go?" Caleb asked. "We don't want to

keep John and James waiting, after all. And I really do want to see Miles' face." His grin threatened to squeeze his ears right off his face.

I hit him playfully in the arm again before hooking my right elbow into his left. We walked out the front door and I was surprised to see a buggy waiting for us.

"Borrowed from Darius Gardner," Caleb answered my questioning glance as he helped me inside. Da took the reins and we headed for town in style.

We drove past the parsonage which answered the question I had forgotten to ask. A few minutes later, Da pulled up in front of the hotel and Caleb hopped out of the buggy and tied up the horses before he helped me down.

When we entered the hotel, a waiter immediately led us to the back and off to a small side room.

"We get our own private dining room?" I whispered to Caleb.

He looked at me and grinned before leading me into the room with Da trailing behind us.

"Happy Birthday!" three voices shouted as we entered.

The sight that greeted me was like one out of the fairy tales Mama had always read to Caleb and me. The table was laden with a feast of food and bouquet upon bouquet of flowers. Three handsome young men in black and dark blue broadcloth suits stood at the other end of the room. The smallest one was half buried by yet another bouquet of flowers.

Miles gave James a gentle push and he stepped forward. He handed me the bouquet of wildflowers.

Once they were out of his hands, he signed the words, "I picked these for you myself." I smiled and, having been rendered speechless, I signed my "thank you" to him. My eyes darted over to where Miles still stared at me.

I saw him swallow hard and glance toward the door where Da looked like he was about ready to run away.

"Iain, it is good to see you here. Thank you for coming." His gaze flitted through the room. "Shall we all sit down, say the blessing, and eat this food instead of just staring at it?"

Caleb let my arm go and gave me a slight shove toward Miles. "Your seat is at the head of the table," he whispered.

Miles pulled the seat of honor out and looked toward me. "Miss Stuart?"

I took first one tentative step and then another toward him until I was around the table and sitting in the chair. He took my bouquet and set it down on a small table behind me.

Dinner was delicious. The conversation was a bit scarce since nobody really knew what to talk about or say. Da didn't say a single word, Caleb looked pleased, but uncomfortable; Miles, James and John tried to be their normal selves. I was still in shock and didn't say much.

After a lovely strawberry preserve tart for dessert, we all sat around, very full and not sure what to do next.

"Thank you all for the best birthday I have ever had," I said.

James grinned and signed his "You're welcome."

Before anyone else could speak, Da stood up

182

and gave Caleb a pointed look. My heart plummeted. Da wanted to leave and he wanted to leave now.

Caleb looked around the table, his eyes hovering over my face for a few extra seconds before landing on Miles. "Miles, could you bring Anna home and return the buggy to the Gardners? Da would like to go home now and I know Anna would probably like to stay." He gave me a wink and I gave him a weak smile back.

"Of course, I can do that," Miles said. "Thank you for joining us, Iain and Caleb. Have a blessed night."

Caleb and Da left, Da in more of a hurry than Caleb. Caleb mussed up John and James' hair and said goodbye before he followed Da out the door.

I knew what Da would be doing as soon as he got home, but I refused to let my mind go there. At least he did it at home rather than at a saloon. Today was my birthday, and I wasn't going to let him ruin it again.

Half an hour later, Miles halted the buggy in front of his house and turned around in his seat. "John, James, this is your stop. Go inside and go to bed. I'll be home soon."

"Can't we go with you?"

"No," Miles said. "You have school tomorrow and need to get some sleep." He glanced over at me, and I tried to hide a smile once I realized what he wasn't saying; he wanted some time alone with me so we could talk without fear of being overheard.

James climbed out of the buggy after giving me a hug from the back and a kiss on the cheek.

"Good night, James," I said. "I'll see you tomorrow afternoon at my house."

As John stomped inside, I said good night to him as well and he waved his hand back at me.

Miles sighed. "Sometimes John reminds me too much of myself."

I turned to him with a raised eyebrow. "How so?"

"Obedient and compliant as long as it goes with what he wants, but as soon as something doesn't go the right way, he is rebellious and moody."

"And are you still that way or is this just how you were when you were his age?"

Miles laughed. "Good question." He clucked to the horses to get them headed to my house. "Mostly when I was his age. Although, I can still revert to those ways on occasion."

I grinned. "I thought so."

"What would you think of dropping the buggy and horses off at the Gardners and then walking back to your house?" he asked after a couple of minutes of silence.

I shrugged. "That would be fine. I wouldn't mind walking off some of this food."

"John asked me this morning when we are getting married."

"What?" I exclaimed.

Miles chuckled. "I told him that it would be at least a few months and then he asked if we would be married before Christmas."

Now I was laughing. "Christmas? That's less than three months away!"

"I know. I told him it might not be until January or later."

I gave a deep breath of relief. "Phew!"

"He was rather disappointed." Miles was looking at me out of the corner of his eyes.

I shook my head. "Of course he was. If he wasn't, I would be worried about him."

Miles threw his head back and laughed, filling the road and surrounding fields with his laughter. When he was done, he took a minute to regain his composure before getting the horses moving again. He sighed and said, "I feel like we are reaching a forked path. Right now, we are on the path where we are friends and only friends—and good ones at that. In a little bit, we are going to reach a fork in that road and we will have to decide do we continue down the road of just friends or do we make the decision that will, ultimately, lead..." he paused and swallowed, "to marriage. And I'm not sure what to do or where to go or how to get there. Or if I want to get there. We've only known each other for almost a year, but I feel like we have been friends forever. And it has been the best year of my life. I don't want that to change."

I put a hand on his arm to stop him from talking. "I don't think it does have to change. Even if we go down the other path, the one that could lead to marriage, we will still be friends. I don't know for sure, but I'm thinking it might be a little uncomfortable for awhile, but we can, and will, still talk to each other as friends and be there for each other. Life will still go on."

Miles stared into my face for an uncomfortable minute before nodding sluggishly. I moved away from him and he clucked to the horses to continue on.

"You always seem to be able to somehow put my mind at ease," Miles said.

185

I was glad for the dark because my cheeks burned. "Only by God's grace," I said.

He reached for my hand and gave it a quick squeeze. "And you hardly ever take the credit for anything."

I grinned and looked over at him. He looked toward me and a moon beam shone through the trees to show the huge grin on his face.

Miles turned his attention back to the road and turned the horses into the Gardner's drive. He pulled right up to the house and Darius waited for us on the porch.

"I wasn't expecting to see you, Miles. If I'd known both of you were coming, I would have had Wilma sit out here with me," Darius said.

"Caleb asked me to bring the buggy here and get his sister home safely," Miles said.

"Did he really say it in that order?"

Miles climbed out of the buggy and helped me down before handing the reins to a grinning Darius. "Here ya go. I think I'd better get Miss Stuart home."

"Yes, Pastor Jenkins," Darius teased with a laugh that followed us down the road.

CHAPTER FIFTEEN

As we walked from the Gardner's to home, I decided to broach the subject of Caleb. "Would you be able to help organize a house raising for Caleb?"

Miles blinked. "Why does he need a house?"

"He's thinking about getting married and Da said he needs to have his own house."

Miles stared at me, confusion written all over his face. "Wait! He's thinking about getting married? Since when?"

"It hasn't been for long. I only found out about it yesterday."

"How long has he been courting this woman?" Miles asked.

"He hasn't. He's been writing to her for about two months."

Miles' confusion deepened. "A mail order bride?"

I nodded.

"And he's thinking about marrying her?"

I nodded again. "I delivered the letter today that asks her to come out here in about four months to meet him, if she still wants to and after he sends her the money. That will give him most of the winter to get the house ready. When she comes, he's going to give her a week or so to decide. If they decide to, they'll marry then.

Miles stared into the distance ahead of us, deep in thought. "Where's that put you after he gets married?"

My mouth went dry as I remembered Da's threat, one I was sure was not empty. "I don't know." I chewed my lower lip. "If Caleb doesn't become a Christian between now and then, I should still be able to stay with Da until...God provides something else. Even if Caleb were to offer to let me stay with him, I probably wouldn't accept after he gets married."

Miles stopped walking and turned in my direction, a look of incredulity just visible on his face in the semi-dark moonlit night. "What did you...? Did you say that if Caleb does NOT become a Christian you'll be able to stay with your pa?"

I avoided eye contact with him and laughed nervously. "Yesterday was a very interesting day. I was accused twice of corrupting people. One person accused me of corrupting John and James in an evil way and another accused me of corrupting Caleb in a good way. Biblically speaking, I mean. Da said that if I 'corrupted' Caleb and he became a Christian, Da would kick me out before I knew what was happening to me."

Miles visibly tensed and his jaw worked back and forth as he tried to keep his mouth shut.

188

"Would he actually do that?"

I nodded.

"Why?"

I leaned against a nearby tree and hugged myself. "Mama was a devout Christian, but Da feels God failed her when Jed was born. Da's the reason I had to stop going to church after Jed turned ten. He felt church was for sissies and Jed was a young man by then. During the next four years, I didn't know God personally, and received no teaching about God. After Jed left I also felt like God had failed us somehow. I became disgruntled with the church people—who didn't really reach out to help me, even right after Mama's death—the townspeople who stuck their noses in the air when I walked by, and worse, I got tired of living. So I didn't go back to church until several months ago when I realized I couldn't do it all on my own, no matter how hard I tried."

"I'm glad you came back. I wish it could have been for different circumstances, but I am glad you came back to church."

"Thank you. I am, too. I never would have found Christ if it weren't for Jed's death. And I never would have found a purpose for my life either. I have truly seen how God's plans are always better than ours, even when we least expect it."

"On another note," he said with a quiet chuckle, "what is your greatest, deepest dream or desire?"

I laughed. "That's easy. I have always wanted to be a wife and mother."

"Always?" He sounded surprised.

"Always. Why do you think I begged Da to

keep Jed? What about you?"

Miles looked sheepish. "Well, when I was younger, I wanted to become a world famous preacher." I smiled at his shy admission. "Now, I just want to be a good dad and follow God's leading with my pastoring." His voice got dreamy as he continued, "I also wanted to have a whole passel of kids." His voice broke. "After James was born, Doc Claybourne said we would never have any more kids. James' muteness was most likely caused by his difficult birth and Rebekah was pregnant when she died." The last admission was said so softly I barely heard it.

Tears welled up in my eyes and my voice refused to work. All I could do was put a comforting hand on his forearm and whisper, "I'm so sorry."

I felt Miles take a deep breath and he cleared his throat. "She and the baby are much happier now than they ever could have been down here and for that I am grateful." He paused to blink his eyes and clear his throat again. "Is there something you would like to know about me? Something no one else might have thought to ask me before?"

"Hmm," I said, putting a finger to my chin. "I'm not sure. Let me think a minute." I searched my memory for something I wanted to know about Miles. It took less than a minute. "If you could have any job in the world, what would it be?"

Miles opened and closed his mouth a few times. "I...that is a good question. I'm not really sure." He was quiet for a few minutes while I watched his face. His jaw worked and his eyes darted around as if searching for the answer in the moonlight. "I would have to say I would still be a pastor. It's always been what I wanted and I don't think that has changed any."

We began to walk again. I had the feeling we were both at a loss for words. It was uncomfortable being in this in-between state. Not quite just friends, but not quite anything deeper, either. We were both unsure of our footing and unsure what to do next.

I was the one to break the silence. "Is there anything you wanted to know about me?"

His answer was almost immediate, "Why did you retreat from society after Jed left?"

My steps faltered just inside the clearing near our house and my breath hitched. "I had very few friends growing up because as soon as school was done, I had to get Jed from the neighbor lady or one of the other women from church, clean the house, do my homework, and make supper. The ladies from church helped me out some, at least for awhile, but by the time I was twelve, I was on my own completely. I had one friend who would come home with me sometimes and help me take care of Jed and clean the house. Sometimes we would do our homework together, too. But after we both were done with school, she wasn't able to come over very much and I was too busy to go over there.

"I don't want to make my da sound like a horrible man, he isn't, but there are some things he did that were very wrong. He blamed Jed for Mama's death. Sometimes I wonder if he blamed Jed more than he blamed God. He hit, beat, or whipped Jed almost every day. If Caleb or I interfered or tried to talk Da out of it, he would take us aside after and threaten us with the same beating or he would sometimes threaten to give Jed twice the beating because we dared to speak up."

I tried to speak with as little emotion as possible, but failed as the tears ran down my cheeks and my voice faltered. I took a deep breath before continuing. "When my friend got married and moved away, I had no more friends left in town and I didn't have time to try to make any new ones. I also had a terrible load of guilt for letting my little brother get beat up every single day. Even though I knew there was nothing I could do about it, I felt like I failed him. I wish I would've told Jed that I tried to stop the beatings. I wish I'd been brave enough to do something. Maybe Jed and I could've run away from here and made a life somewhere else. I don't know. I wish I could've done something. After he ran off, my guilt increased and I felt like everybody in town would judge me. They might not've known what had happened, and they certainly didn't know that I thought I was at fault, but I still felt as if they were judging me."

My tears escaped my closed eyelids faster, and I didn't try to stop them anymore. Sobs tried to wrack my body, but I managed to steel myself against them.

Miles was quiet and I wondered what he was thinking about what I had said. Was he the type of man who hated it when women cried? Did he get uncomfortable and... The thought flew right out of my head as his arm wrapped around my shoulder and he pulled me closer to him.

I stiffened when his hand touched my opposite shoulder, but he whispered softly, "You can cry, Anna. I can't imagine how hard that must have been for you. And if I'm not mistaken, you haven't expressed your feelings on this before or shared them with others. You have a lot of pent-up emotions trapped in you."

I nodded, my head hitting his shoulder. "How do you know me so well?" I asked in a hoarse voice.

"God."

We were both quiet for a minute until my tears slowed down. "Thank you." I pulled away from his comforting embrace.

"That's what friends are for," Miles said, a smile sounding in his voice. "Friends are there to provide a shoulder to cry into as well as being a shoulder to lean on."

I smiled and a small laugh escaped my lips. "It's nice to have a friend again. Well, two, I guess. You and Wilma."

"What about the boys?" Miles asked with a twinkle in his eyes.

I swatted him. "They're a different kind of friend. More of a...well...more of a mother-son relationship." My cheeks flamed when I realized what I had said.

"That's a good thing," Miles said. "Even if we don't end up getting married, they still need to have a mother figure in their lives." Miles led me to the porch at the front of our house. "It's getting late and I suppose I should head home and make sure the boys are in bed."

I paused at the bottom of the step to the front door. "Yes, you should. Thank you for being a shoulder to cry into today, Miles."

"You're welcome, Anna. Anytime you need another shoulder, let me know," he said with a wink. "And thank you for giving me some real, deep adult conversation for the first time in the last two years."

"You're welcome. I was happy to oblige. I will see you tomorrow for supper, correct?"

"Yes, ma'am. I wouldn't miss your cooking for the world."

I blushed. "See you then." I opened the door and stepped into the dark house.

Miles watched Anna until the door closed behind her. He hoped Caleb had her da in bed by now. He knew Iain had gone home to do some drinking and prayed Anna wouldn't have to deal with that on her birthday. He turned away and started walking toward home.

When he reached the road, he looked around. Seeing no one, he prayed out loud. "Dear heavenly Father, You know my innermost thoughts before I know what they are. You are the All-knowing One, Jehovah-Jireh, the Lord who provides. Lord, You are the Lord of all Wisdom. I am in desperate need of wisdom right now. I can't figure this out on my own and I know I am not supposed to even try to. Lord, what am I supposed to do? That fork in the road is coming faster and faster. I don't want to get there too fast, but I feel my feet trying to run faster. Are Anna and I supposed to be just friends or do You have more planned for us than that? I always thought people were given only one chance at love and one perfect mate. I thought Rebekah was that one. Now..." He stopped to gather his thoughts and let a wagon with a late night traveler rattle past him.

"Now, I am starting to have feelings for Anna. Is it simply because she is the first person—the first woman—who has broken through the defenses I built up after Rebekah's death? Or is this really something else? Am I really falling in love with her or not? And then there is the ultimatum from Iain. God, what am I supposed to do about that? I know Caleb will do everything he can, but if Iain kicks Anna out and Caleb can't do anything..." He drew in a deep breath and let it out slowly. "Lord, lead me in the path You desire for me and do not let me stray. I need Your wisdom, O Lord. As Anna's favorite hymn says, 'Be Thou My Wisdom, O Lord of my heart.'" He stopped at the edge of the church property. "Guide me as I learn to walk this new path. In Jesus' name, Amen."

CHAPTER SIXTEEN

The rest of the week went by in a blur. After the excitement on Monday, John and James seemed to decide it was time to misbehave as much as possible. Although Miles disciplined them, they still did not want to listen to me. On Friday, I was at my wits end. Neither of them had done any of their chores that week and instead of doing their homework, they were goofing off.

"John Carlton Jenkins!" I yelled above the racket they were making.

John stared at me with wide eyes. I wasn't sure if it was my use of his middle name or the raised voice that got his attention. Whatever it was, it worked. "John, go get your school books, sit at the table and do your homework right now. You will not get anything to eat or play with until you do and you absolutely will not be coming out to our farm tomorrow."

I turned my head to James. "James Miles Jenkins, you get yourself into the living room and pick up the entire mess that was made in there. The same threats apply to you. If switchings and scoldings from your father won't work, we'll go with other things instead." They both stared at me as if I were a stranger. "Git!" I said, a stern and determined look etched into my face.

The only problem I had with splitting them up, was that I couldn't split myself into two pieces to make sure they did what I told them to. All I could do was work on supper in the kitchen and wander into the living room every few minutes. They both dawdled and I knew it was because they thought their father would be lenient.

As five o'clock rolled around, I stepped onto the porch to wait for Miles. When I opened the door, I breathed in the fresh, cool autumn air for the first time that afternoon. I closed my eyes and breathed deeply, savoring the scents of the leaves and dirt in the air. I sank into the porch swing and pushed it into slow motion.

I was only there for a few minutes when the sound of whistling came up the road. I kept my eyes closed and smiled as I listened to Miles whistling "And Can it Be?" It hadn't taken me long to realize that was his favorite hymn. When his footsteps fell lightly on the first step, I opened my eyes.

"What's this?" he asked.

"We need to talk before you go inside," I said.

Miles moved over to stand in front of me. He leaned back onto the porch railing and crossed his arms. "Now what?"

"Same as all week. They won't do their chores or homework. What I need to tell you is that you need to be firm tonight. I told them that they don't

198

get any food or play time until they are finished. And if they still aren't finished, they won't be coming to the farm tomorrow. I hope I'm not over stepping my bounds..."

Miles shook his head, interrupting me. "Not at all. Perhaps missing a meal will help them realize they are wrong. It is a good idea and one I hadn't thought of."

I smiled and stood up. "Thank you."

"Before you leave, can I talk to you for a minute?"

I paused in my movement. "That would be fine," I said, unsure what he would say.

"I've been doing a lot of thinking this week and I'd like to talk to you on Sunday night. Could you and I take a walk sometime in the evening? Maybe Caleb could spend some time with the boys at our...my place."

I blinked my eyes a few times and my throat felt dry. What was he thinking about? Did this have something to do with the fork in the road he talked about on Monday? I swallowed hard. "Sure, we should be able to do that. I know Caleb would be fine with it. What time would you like us to be here?"

"How about right after supper?" Miles' face was a study of relief and anxious worry.

All I could do was nod. When I got my voice working again, I said, "Could you tell the boys goodbye for me, please?"

Miles nodded. "And I'll make sure they get their homework and chores done. If they don't show up by nine tomorrow morning, you'll know they didn't get it done and they will spend their time with me tomorrow. I'll think up some creative chores for them to do." He winked at me and I smiled back.

"Good! I will see you on Sunday, then." I stepped off the porch and waved back at him. "Bye!"

"Goodbye, Anna," Miles said in a soft voice. "God bless you."

After Da went to bed for the night that Sunday, Caleb and I walked to the parsonage. Miles was waiting for us on the porch.

"The boys are inside setting up a game for you three to play," Miles told Caleb.

Caleb gave a sheepish grin. "I hope I know how to play it."

Miles chuckled. "It's not very hard and you probably don't know it since they made it up."

Caleb gave a mock groan and slowly opened the door as if expecting something to explode on the other side.

Miles stepped off the porch. "Would you rather walk or sit here on the porch swing?" he asked as he joined me.

"Let's walk," I said. At least then, I could let off some of my nervous energy. Hopefully. Miles was silent as we approached the woods on the other side of the road. In the silence, my thoughts ran wild.

We'd been courting for almost six months. Was this talk about that? I thought it had been going well. Was I wrong? Or was this a different kind of talk? I tried not to look as nervous as I felt while I waited for Miles to say whatever it was he wanted to say.

After what seemed like an eternity, Miles cleared his throat and let out a shaky breath. "I never knew saying something like this could be so hard." He looked at his hands. "I think our relationship needs to change. I know we've been courting for about six months now. I'd always believed the best way to court was to get to know someone for a couple of years before getting married. Maybe even before courting. Now...I'm not so sure. I'm not getting any younger. I'm 32, going on 33. We have a good, solid friendship based on our mutual belief in God and growing faith in Him." He paused and took a deep breath.

I looked at the trees, the faint outlines of the birds, was that a squirrel's nest? It was too dark to tell. I looked everywhere to, toward, or near Miles. After being nervous he would break off the courtship, I was now nervous he was going to propose. Tonight.

I glanced at him out of the corner of my eye, trying to keep my breath even and calm as we neared the top of a small hill.

"I've prayed so much about this that God is probably tired of me talking to Him," Miles continued with a nervous laugh. "About two months ago, God impressed on me I was supposed to marry you. I pushed it aside assuming it was because of John's and James' insistence about it, coming to me while I prayed. Then it happened again. And again. And again. Day after day it kept coming to me. Finally, I prayed and asked God if that was from Him. Although I didn't hear it audibly, it seemed like He said, 'Yes, marry Anna. Now.' That was a month ago. I kept praying and asking God if I heard him right. I know I shouldn't do that." He gave a short, forced laugh. "After all, I'm the pastor, I'm not supposed to doubt God's Word, right?"

I shook my head. "You may be a pastor, but that doesn't make you infallible."

Miles relaxed a little and gave a small smile. "Thank you, Anna." Even after he relaxed, he still refused to look at me. I wondered if he was as nervous as I was. Out of the corner of my eye, I saw him close his eyes and swallow hard.

"Saturday, I prayed all day about us and what we should do. God was very insistent the whole day that I was to marry you. Not later. Not in one or two years. I probably should have warned you a little more than this so you could be praying about it more, but I'm hoping and praying you were already doing so."

I closed my eyes. Was he really saying what I thought he was saying?

Miles shifted his feet in a pile of dry leaves. I felt his presence leave my side and wondered what he was doing. Then he put his hand over mine. My eyes flew open. Miles knelt in front of me.

"Anna, I first started falling in love with you the day you marched up to me with my two boys. I'd heard about you from them, especially James, and had watched you with them sometimes, but that was the first time I had actually truly seen you in all your righteous anger." Miles chuckled as his fingers played with mine. "That was the first time I really talked to you. Before, I had only talked at you, but that time I talked to you."

He took a deep breath. "I'm getting off topic. My point in all this is to say I love you and cannot imagine living the rest of my life without you. Anna, will you marry me?"

I took a shaky breath and swallowed hard. "Yes," I whispered. I cleared my throat. "As long as you are sure. I still don't think I will be a good pastor's wife."

"And I believe you will be a wonderful pastor's wife. You are caring, gentle, and kind. You love people, care for them, and can relate to both genuine Christians and those who think they are Christians, but don't have a genuine relationship with Christ. As someone who came to that knowledge later in life, you can relate to the works-oriented Christians more easily and they can relate to you.

"Whenever I share my testimony, I have to tell them I became a Christian when I was six and grew up in the church. With you, you can tell them you became a genuine Christian when you were thirty and they will more readily listen to you because you didn't grow up in the church. There are some advantages and disadvantages to both. But all-in-all, I think you will make the perfect pastor's wife even if all you do is raise my sons and any children we might have together."

I nodded.

"I have never been more sure of anything in my life. God was practically taking a tree limb to my head and hitting me with it, trying to get me to finally propose to you."

I grinned. "I would have liked to see that."

Miles grimaced. "I'm sure you would have."

We walked along in silence until we reached

the clearing James had led me to so many months ago. It was hard to believe it had been over a year since I had first met John and James.

"When should we tell the boys?" I asked as I stepped around a stump.

I looked back at Miles and saw a mischievous look light up his face. "I think we should make them guess it. Although, once they see the ri..." his eyes grew wide. "I forgot to give you the ring!" He dug quickly in his right pants pocket. "There it is. Your left hand please, Miss Stuart."

I chuckled and gave him my left hand. He slipped the simple gold band on my fourth finger. "There," he said with triumph. "Now we can make them figure it out on their own."

He kept hold of my hand and gently guided our path back the way we had come.

When we arrived at Miles' house, there was a note on the kitchen table for us. "The boys are in bed and I have gone home. Miles, can you please make sure Anna arrives home safely? Caleb"

"Perhaps we should wait until Tuesday night when we are all together?" Miles asked.

"Did you ask their permission first?"

Miles nodded.

"Caleb will notice the ring tomorrow morning. Da probably will, too, though he won't say anything."

"What are you saying?"

I took a deep breath. "I don't know. I guess

I'm saying I can tell my family. We can both tell John and James tomorrow morning."

"Tell us what?" a young male voice asked from the stairs.

Miles clenched his jaw. "You boys are supposed to be in bed." His voice held a note of carefully controlled anger. Without turning around, I knew I would see both boys sitting on the stairs, watching and listening to us. "Upstairs, both of you," Miles commanded. "Now!"

"You wouldn't have to wait until morning..." John started.

"You're right, we wouldn't," Miles said. "I think we will wait at least until Tuesday." Miles looked at me with a question on his face and I nodded in agreement. "I will also be thinking of another way to punish you two for all your disobedience this week. Get upstairs and go to bed. If you aren't asleep by the time I get back from Anna's, I will get more creative."

I turned around to see their reaction, keeping my left hand out of sight.

Both boys had their heads hanging. "Yes, Pa," John said.

They trudged up the stairs and Miles and I left.

As we walked down the road, Miles gave a deep sigh. "I don't know what to do about those two."

I chewed my bottom lip. "I know telling them that we are engaged will help them behave, but I think it would almost be a reward if we told them. And I think we both want them to learn from this week of rebellion and disobedience and to start obeying without something like an engagement helping them."

"Yes, but in the meantime, how do we get them to learn this?"

"The chicken coop needs cleaning before winter," I said with a mischievous grin on my face.

Miles threw his head back and laughed. "That would work. Tuesday or tomorrow? I know they're usually at your place on Tuesday."

"Tuesday would work fine. But, we'll tell them what they will be doing tomorrow." I thought for a long minute. "How about cleaning the windows and airing out the beds and bedding? Could we keep them out of school tomorrow and Tuesday?"

Miles' head turned sharply toward me. "Do you think that would be a punishment?"

"Yes, I do. They enjoy school, if not for the schooling, then for their friends."

"Hm," Miles grunted. "As long as you're up to it."

I grinned. "Don't worry, I've got plans racing through my mind already."

We turned into my yard. My yard. It wouldn't be my yard for long. I swallowed hard and tried to settle the butterflies that suddenly fluttered in my stomach. As we reached the porch, Miles took my hand and gave it a lingering kiss.

"Good night, Anna. I will see you tomorrow."

"Good night, Miles."

I stood on the porch and watched his retreating back until it was lost in the shadows and then I headed inside.

CHAPTER SEVENTEEN

The next morning, I rose early and prepared biscuits and gravy for breakfast. I still wore my engagement ring, although I knew I had to leave it home for the day. I wanted Caleb and Da to notice it. I still couldn't believe I was engaged. It seemed to have happened so quickly, but I knew it was the right thing to do. Even as I admitted that, a doubtful thought came to my mind. Was I truly in love with Miles? Yes, I believed I was. But what was love of a man supposed to be like? Was I supposed to feel differently?

Oh, Mama, how I wish you were still around to help guide me! I don't know what to think or do. My hands froze as a thought hit me. Wilma. Wilma would know. My mind raced. When would I be able to see her? I could go there tomorrow morning before the boys came, I decided.

Caleb came inside from chores and sat heavily in the chair.

"You do that too many times and it'll break

right under you one of these days," I teased.

"Naw," he protested. "I built this chair. It'll withstand a little beating now and again."

"If you say so."

"How was your walk with Miles?" Caleb asked as Da stepped in the house and sat down to eat.

"Good," I said, not meeting his eyes as I dished up the biscuits, gravy, and sausage.

When I gave him his plate, Caleb took my left hand off the gravy and sausage bowl. "What's this?" he asked, a twinkle in his eye.

"A ring," I answered, fighting off the grin that threatened to break out on my face.

Da's fork stopped midway to his mouth. "He really did it, then, did he? Miles asked me daughter to marry him?"

I turned to him. "Yes, Da, he did."

Da grunted and returned to his food. After taking another bite, he said, "He does know what he is getting himself into, doesn't he?"

"What do you mean, Da?"

"He knows how short-tempered you can be, how much you like to control things, how stubborn you are, and that you ain't really pastor's wife material?"

I nodded. "Yes, Da, he knows that is how I used to be. Now that I am a genuine Christian, I have changed though and he thinks I will make a good pastor's wife. I'm not quite sure I believe him, but he thinks it is so."

Da grunted again, but didn't speak.

"I think you'll make a wonderful pastor's wife," Caleb said. "Though, I bet there's a few women in church who won't like it one bit."

I groaned as I sank into my chair. "I'm sure you're right about that last one."

The rest of the meal was silent as we all ate. Da left as soon as he had finished and Caleb mopped up the last of his gravy with another biscuit. After gulping down his milk, he slid his chair back.

"Congratulations, Anna," he said. "I'm happy for you."

I smiled up at him. "Thank you, Caleb."

Caleb nodded and followed Da out the door. I cleaned up quickly and started planning out the day. Glancing up at the clock, I was surprised by how late it was. I looked at the sink full of dishes and decided to leave them until tonight. I rushed to my room, took my ring off, and hurried out the door and down the road.

I was out of breath by the time I got to the parsonage. By the look on Miles' face when he stepped out on the porch to greet me, I knew things were already going sour this morning. "What happened?" I asked.

Miles raised an eyebrow. "How did you know?"

I grinned. "Your face, Mr. Jenkins, told me something wasn't going well today."

Miles sighed and closed his eyes. "Good luck with them today, Anna. I don't know what to do anymore. They were getting a little wild and disobedient before you stepped in. Then they had a few months when they were doing so well. Now this. I'm not sure what to do. I've been praying about it, but I feel like God isn't answering my prayers. I've talked to them, used lack of food, switchings, everything I can think of, and none of it has curbed their rebellion and outright disobedience."

My breath caught in my chest and an odd sensation came over me. As Miles spoke, something asked me, "What did you read this morning?" When he finished talking, I said, "Do you have your Bible?"

Miles looked confused, but handed me his Bible. I took it and flipped toward the back of the Bible. "Here it is. 'For we wrestle not against flesh and blood, but against principalities, against powers, against the rulers of the darkness of this world, against spiritual wickedness in high places.' Could it be Satan feels threatened by you and is attacking you by using your sons?"

The look on Miles' face was indescribable. I couldn't tell if it was shock, amazement, or revelation. Whatever it was, it took him a minute to get out of his stupor. "I never thought of that." He looked off into the distance. "Thank you, Anna. I am constantly amazed how God has used you in my life and the lives around you."

I looked away. "I should probably go in and see what kind of trouble they are getting into."

Miles put a gentle hand on my arm as I brushed past him. "I'll be praying for you and the boys and for Satan to stay away today."

I nodded. "Thank you."

Miles let go of my arm and walked across the yard to the church.

I took a deep breath and opened the door. I thought I was prepared for everything, but I found out I wasn't. John held a pile of blankets and was already headed for the back door which James held open for him. "Thank you, Jesus," I prayed.

By the time they came back inside, I had a

smile on my face and my sleeves rolled up. "What's the plan, boys?" John and James looked over at me, blinking their eyes in confusion. "Okay, fine, I guess I'll have to tell you. The plan for today is to get the mattresses and bedding aired out. After that is done, we will wash the windows. Sound good?"

My statement was met with silence. I raised an eyebrow and gave a sharp nod. "Okay, then. It looks like you've already gotten started, so how about we start by getting the mattresses outside. Then you two can have fun whacking the quilts and mattresses." Still no response from them, either negative or positive. I heaved a silent sigh. It appeared they had decided to use the silent treatment.

Together, we walked upstairs and, with me on one end and the two boys on the other, we maneuvered the mattresses out of the rooms, down the stairs, through the kitchen, and outside. We rested one mattress on its side against one of the clothesline poles and another mattress on the other pole. Miles' mattress was leaned against the side of the house. It was too big and heavy to move any further. When the mattresses were outside, I sent the boys off to find some good sized sticks.

While I draped the blankets over the clothesline, I compared this work day with the first one we'd had. The only thing that was the same was that we were all three hard at work in the same house. "God, please help me get through to these boys today." I began to hum some hymns. As I finished hanging the last blanket, my humming turned to low singing. After I got some water warming up to wash windows with, the volume of my singing went up and I was singing at full volume.

When the boys came in from beating the bedding, I was singing Miles' favorite hymn, "And Can it Be?" Without looking back, I told the boys, "There's a rag for each of you in the bucket."

I heard water splash a little and knew they were listening again. As I moved on to "Amazing Grace" I looked over at them and knew I had to say something.

"John, James, come here please." I waited until they stood in front of me. "I know what you are trying to do by not saying anything, but you do know that you aren't really punishing anyone except yourselves, don't you? Your subtle rebellion, while it does affect me and your father, it only frustrates us. But with you, if you allow your anger to fester, it will affect you for the rest of your life."

I took a deep breath and crouched down to their level. "It was festering anger that caused Da to lash out at Jed. It was festering anger that got my youngest brother killed for the crimes he had committed.

"If you continue on the way you have been and reject what God has clearly told you in the Bible and through your father's words, your anger will turn you into young men you would never recognize."

I turned back to the window I had been washing to let my words sink in. As I washed, I prayed God would use my words and Satan would leave this house and these two young boys alone.

There wasn't much of a change in them that day except they did eventually start talking and signing. I prayed things would be better the next day when they were cleaning out the chicken coop.

As I had left the night before, Miles had promised he would have the boys out the door no later than half past seven. If all went well today, Miles would announce our engagement tonight at supper. Before they arrived I had to gather a few tools.

The wheelbarrow, shovels, and handkerchiefs were ready for use by the time they arrived.

"Lads," I said with a dramatic gesture toward the coop, "this is a chicken coop. Not only is it a chicken coop, it is a chicken coop that is in desperate need of unburying, cleaning and scrubbing." At this point, I heard two stifled giggles. Trying not to join in, I continued my grand tour. "This," picking up a shovel, "is the implement that shall be used for the daring task. These handkerchiefs will be put over your mouths and noses to keep you from suffocating while you work. And this barrow is for transporting the vile substances from the coop to the manure pile. Any questions?"

John raised his hand.

"Yes, Sir John?"

"Who's doing what?"

"An excellent question. Methinks we shall have both of you shoveling the vile substances out into the wheelbarrow. After it has been filled, I shall transport it to the manure pile and bring the wheelbarrow back for refilling. While I am away, you can each clean out a nesting box of the hay. Yes, Sir James?"

"Why can't we transport the wheelbarrow?" he signed.

"It would be awfully heavy," I said.

"We don't have to fill it all the way," James protested.

I nodded. "Would you like to do that? The two of you could take turns pushing the wheelbarrow and filling it then."

James nodded his head vigorously. John looked between the two of us and shrugged.

"This way you can get other things done," James signed.

I smiled. *Lord, is James starting to come back?* "Thank you, James. If you need help, I will be in the garden preparing it for winter."

That day went much smoother than the day before. There was actually some banter and even a few joyful noises. Ever since I met them, I had wondered how there could be banter when one boy couldn't speak but James made up for it somehow. They even got into arguments once in awhile. I still hadn't quite figured that one out.

They were still hard at work scrubbing the chicken coop when Miles came in the house to find me. "How did it go?" he asked.

"Look for yourself," I said, nodding toward the open back door.

Miles looked out the door. "Is that John singing?"

I grinned. "Yes, it is. He's been doing that all afternoon. James makes a suggestion and John sings it."

Miles looked at me with wonder in his eyes. "Thank the Lord! Does this mean we can finally announce our engagement to them?"

214

I got suddenly shy and nodded.

"You don't know how hard it has been the last couple of days not being able to tell them," Miles said. "It seems like there is always an opportunity when I could, but I couldn't because they weren't deserving of knowing yet."

A grin played at the corners of my mouth. "We could always make them wait another week."

Miles' eyes grew wide. "No! Please don't!"

Our laughter must have reached all the way outside because next thing we knew, there was a shout, "Pa's here!" and the patter of running feet. Miles was practically tackled to the floor, but he somehow managed to stay upright.

"What is this?" Miles asked.

"Pa, James and I have something to say to you and Miss Stuart," John said in a serious voice.

"Oh?"

James nodded and signed, "We've been very bad the last week. I am sorry."

"I'm sorry, too, Pa and Miss Stuart. I know we've been nearly impossible to deal with and I know that having to stay home from school and do all this cleaning was part of the punishment. Even if parts of it were fun, I still think it did what you wanted it to do."

James clapped his hands, interrupting his brother. He signed, "What Miss Stuart said yesterday helped the most though, I think."

"What did Miss Stuart say?" Miles asked.

"That our rebellion would only hurt us in the long run, not you and her," John answered. "And that we were rejecting what you and God had clearly told us to do."

215

Miles nodded and gave me a smile. "You are both forgiven. I am very grateful that you realized your mistakes."

"I also forgive you both," I said, tears threatening to spill out of my eyelids.

James ran to me and gave me a big hug while John gave his father a hug.

"You boys finished with the chicken coop?" Miles asked.

"Not quite," John answered.

"Then how about you go finish it?" I said, wrinkling my nose. "Besides, you two stink. When you're done, go take a rinse in the creek."

"Yes, ma'am," they both responded with a grin.

"I'm glad they still had more to do," Miles said after they were out of earshot. "We need to at least talk about when we want to have the wedding. Because I know those two will want to know how long they have to wait."

I laughed and cubed potatoes. "They certainly will. Since Christmas is coming up so fast, I think we should definitely wait until after Christmas."

"Plus we need to find someone to officiate for us and to take the pulpit for a Sunday. I intend to take you on at least a short honeymoon trip."

I paused in my cutting and turned to look at Miles. "You do?"

Miles smiled a bit shyly. "Yes, I do."

I turned my back on him again to hide my flaming cheeks. "How about early February?" I

216

asked, trying to keep my voice calm and even.

Miles was quiet for a minute and I was about to turn around to find out why when Caleb's voice cut in, "Unless you wanted to do a double wedding when Maggie gets here."

I spun around. "When did you sneak in?"

Caleb grinned and shrugged. "The door was wide open."

"And anyway," I continued, "When is Maggie going to be here?"

"I don't know for sure. I told her about four months which would be the end of February or beginning of March," Caleb replied.

"I think early February would be better for us," Miles said. "Now that I'm engaged, I'd kind of like to hurry it up. I like Anna helping take care of the boys, but I think it will be better once she is my wife and legally their step-mother."

Caleb's grin widened. "It was only an idea."

"Early February, then," Miles said.

I checked the potatoes that were frying in butter, garlic, and salt. The chicken had already been frying for almost an hour and I used my knife to check it.

Turning back to the men who were now talking quietly to each other, I interrupted them. "Caleb, is Da about ready for supper?"

"Almost. I'll go check on the boys and help them finish up."

"Is there something I can do?" Miles asked.

"You could set the table," I suggested.

"It looks like we need plates and forks, correct?"

I smiled. "Yes. The cupboard to the left of the

sink and the drawer under the counter next to the sink." I answered his question before he asked it.

When the rest of the men got in, the table was set and the food was on the table.

As was usual for our Tuesday evening meals, Miles prayed a blessing over the food and everybody started eating, but there was no conversation until I asked a question.

"How did the chicken coop cleaning go, John and James?"

"Great!" John exclaimed. "We got it all out of there and scrubbed. We do need to get some hay in the nesting boxes after supper, though. Even with Caleb coming out to help us, we didn't quite have enough time."

I smiled. It sure was good to hear some enthusiasm from John again.

"I am proud of you boys for getting it done and for doing it cheerfully," Miles said.

"It'll be good bragging rights, too," John said with a grin. "We can tell everybody at school that we cleaned out a chicken coop."

The corners of Miles' mouth twitched. "Just remember what Proverbs says, 'Pride goeth before destruction, and an haughty spirit before a fall.' You don't want to be proud about your accomplishments."

"Yes, Pa," John said. "I'll try."

Miles looked at me with a question in his eyes and my heart fluttered and a lump formed in my throat, but I gave him the nod he was looking for.

"Now, I know Iain and Caleb already know, but I think it is time for John and James to know and for us to make it official. Would you two like to know what I am talking about?"

John and James were practically wriggling out of their chairs in excitement and Miles was enjoying the suspense way too much.

"What is it, Pa?" John finally asked.

"I don't know. Caleb, should we tell them yet or should we make 'em wait?"

Caleb tried to keep a straight face as he looked from John to James to me and back to Miles. He shrugged. "Good question." He leaned his right elbow on the table and put his chin in his hand. "I think we should make 'em wait until after we've finished eating dessert."

Miles chuckled. "Okay, we'll wait until after dessert then." He took a big bite of chicken and chewed with slow, deliberate movements of his jaw and teeth.

James tried to glare at his father, but Miles refused to look at either of his sons. He finally resorted to clapping his hands to get Miles' attention.

"Yes, Mr. James?" Miles asked.

"You're not being very nice," James signed.

I couldn't help myself. A big laugh escaped my mouth and Da glared at me.

"What's so funny, Anna?" Da asked gruffly.

"James is reprimanding his da for not being nice."

"Humph," Da grunted. "James is right. Just tell the lads, Preacher. All ye'll do is get 'em riled up and I willna have riled up boys in me house."

A light sparked in Miles' eyes and his jaw clenched. "My boys don't get riled up, Mr. Stuart," he said, his voice deceptively calm. "They may get a bit anxious, but they'll not get riled up."

I tried to find a way to lighten the mood again. In a few short seconds, the intensity level had risen much too high. My mind went blank when the look on John's face registered in my mind.

The same light that had sparked in Miles' eyes was also in John's, but in John it appeared more dangerous. His chest heaved in quick, short breaths as if he'd had the wind knocked out of him and he was trying to catch his breath. His small fists were clenched and he stared at Da with an intensity that scared me.

"John," I whispered. "Be slow to anger."

He looked over at me and unshed tears glistened in his eyes. He pursed his lips and gave a quick nod. He took a bite of potatoes, chewed them, and swallowed them. "These are real good potatoes, Miss Stuart. "

I smiled in spite of the mood in the room. "Thank you, John. I'm glad you like them. Do you like them, too, James?"

James gave me a half-smile and nodded.

"Good!" Miles exclaimed. "Because you'll have to put up with her cooking until you move out."

All movement in the room stopped except Da's fork stabbing another potato chunk and Miles' mouth turning up its corners.

John flitted his eyes between Miles and me. "Are you really going to get married?"

I nodded and Miles said, "Yes, we are."

"Yippee!! We get a new ma!" John shouted. He shot a look down the table, daring Da to protest.

James clapped his hands in excitement and the grin on his face proved he was as happy as his

220

brother.

"When's the wedding?" John asked.

"February at the earliest," Miles answered.

"February?" John protested.

"Yes, February," I said. "There are a lot of things that need to be taken care of before we can get married. And we need to figure out who can marry us."

John gave a dramatic sigh. "Okay. I'll try to be patient."

I looked over at James. "I can wait patiently, but I will definitely look forward to it," James signed. I smiled at him.

"You might be able to wait, but I can't," John protested. "February's still..." he counted, "...almost four months away!"

Caleb chuckled. "Would it help to know I might be getting married shortly after your da and my sister do?"

John's eyes went wide and he stumbled on his words. "What? To who?"

"Whom," I corrected.

"That's what I said," John protested. "To whom?"

"To a young woman from Ohio. She has a daughter about the same age as you, John."

John made a face. "A girl? Blech! Why couldn't she have a son?"

Miles laughed. "If there were no girls, there would be no women. And if there were no women, there would be no children. It's a fact of life, my boy."

John wrinkled his nose. "If you say so. But I think God could've figured out a different way of

221

doing things."

Da slammed his fork on the table. "I'm goin' out to finish the chores. I'll do yours, Caleb, so you can join in all this religious talk."

"But we weren't talking about religion," John protested.

I put a hand on John's arm. When he looked my way, I gave a stern shake of my head.

"You most certainly were, Boy!" Da said. "And I don't hafta listen to it either."

He stomped out of the room and the room remained silent for a minute until James clapped his hands for attention. "What's Caleb's bride's name?" he signed.

"Maggie McDougall," I said.

"And her daughter's name?" John asked.

"Rachel," Caleb answered.

"I suppose we have to be nice to her," John stated.

Miles raised an eyebrow. "Yes, you do. Once Caleb and Maggie are married and Anna and I are married, you and Rachel will be cousins."

"Cousins with a girl?" John was aghast.

I cleared my throat and tried not to laugh. Exchanging a twinkling look with Miles I said, "What if your da and I have a baby girl sometime after we're married? Would you protest so loud then at having a sister?"

John's eyes went as wide as tea saucers. "A sister?"

Caleb chuckled. "Sisters aren't too bad. They can cook and clean and sew clothes for you."

"I thought that's what ma's were for," John said.

"Ma's get tired sometimes," Caleb answered. Then he looked down at the table. "Or sometimes they die. Then sisters have to take over."

"Really?"

"Or girl cousins," Caleb said, looking up with a wink. John groaned.

I looked over at James and barely caught the sparkle in his eye. He was loving this conversation. "I can't wait to have a girl cousin and possibly a baby sister, too," he signed.

I grinned at him. "Good," I signed back.

"Well, boys, I suppose we should head home. You two still have a little homework to do ."

"Okay, Pa." John said. "When do we get to meet Mrs. McDougall, Caleb?"

"Probably the Sunday after she arrives. I don't know for sure," Caleb replied.

"Okay. When is she coming?"

"I don't know for sure yet as I haven't heard."

"Will you let us know?"

Caleb smiled and nodded. "Yes, I will."

"Okay, that's enough questions for tonight, John. Say your goodbyes and let's go," Miles said.

"Goodbye, Caleb, Miss Stuart," John said with a wave of his hand. "When can...?"

"No more questions," Miles exclaimed.

James gave me a hug and the three Jenkins men left our house.

"Are you sure you want to be John's mother?" Caleb asked.

I laughed and started to clean up. "Yes, I am."

Caleb shook his head and went outside to help Da with the chores while I cleaned up the rest of supper before going to bed.

CHAPTER EIGHTEEN

Despite all my attempts to visit Wilma, I didn't manage to talk to her until Sunday when she and Darius walked to church with Caleb and me. I stole her away from her husband and pulled her back away from the two men.

Wilma looked at me in surprise and said, "What is all this about?"

"I had to tell you before it was announced at church," I said. I could hardly believe how breathless and excited I was. "I'm engaged!"

Wilma's eyes went wide and she stopped in her tracks. "You are? To Pastor Jenkins?"

I nodded and at my first head bob, Wilma squealed, causing the two men to turn their head back toward us. Caleb whispered something to Darius and he chuckled as he gave a quick nod of understanding.

"Congratulations, Anna! I am so happy for you! You'll have to tell me all about it after church because then the old biddies can't chew you out."

I tried not to laugh, but I couldn't help myself. "Old biddies? Wilma Gardner, where did you get that term from?"

"It's what my mother called them sometimes. Actually, I heard one of them use the term for herself and her group of friends."

"Hmm. I could see us doing that when we are old and decrepit."

Wilma's silvery laugh reached to all the corners of the woods we were walking through. "Except, even when you are old and decrepit, you will still be a pastor's wife and will need to be a good example to all those around you. And, therefore, you can't go around being an old biddy."

We laughed together and caught up to Caleb and Darius as we reached the church yard and we went our separate ways for the church service.

During the sermon, I tried to listen, but I knew Miles would be announcing our engagement at the end of the service and grew more and more nervous as the sermon went on. When he finally finished with a prayer of blessing, I was a nervous wreck. The palms of my hands were clammy, sweat trickled down under the high collar of my new dress, and my heart raced faster than the fastest thoroughbred.

"Before you leave for the day, I do have an announcement to make. I know it will come as a shock to many of you, especially those who have known me the longest. If my assumption is correct, most of you probably heard the rumor that I have been courting someone for a few months. After much prayer, and getting to know her better, I believe God is leading me to marry her. Last Sunday evening, I asked a lovely young woman to become my wife and she said yes." Light applause sprinkled through the congregation and Miles held up his hand for silence. His grin widened. "I can't honestly tell you who is more excited, me and her, or my two boys."

"What's the name of this wonder woman who stole your heart?" a male voice called out.

Miles smiled. He was having fun with the suspense again, but I prayed he knew if he let it go too long, one of the older ladies, like Mrs. Morgan, would say something.

"Anna Stuart." And he left it at that.

Murmurs rippled through the congregation and people turned in their seats to look back at me.

"Thank you for coming today," Miles said. "May the Lord bless you and keep you as you enter your mission field this week. You are dismissed."

Miles made his way to the back to shake hands with those who had attended the service and on his way past the pew in which I was sitting, he beckoned for me to come with him. We had not discussed this and I sat frozen for a few seconds until my brother elbowed me.

I stood up and walked over to join Miles. "What am I supposed to do?" I whispered to him as the first congregant approached.

"All you have to do is smile and shake people's hands," Miles whispered back. "Say something nice if you feel like responding."

Most everybody was polite as they left the church, though I could have sworn Mrs. Morgan tried to murder me with her gaze. After everybody had left, I discreetly shook out and stretched my arm and hand. Miles chuckled under his breath. "How do you do this every week?" I asked.

"After a few weeks, your arm gets used to it."

I rolled my eyes. "Sure. Just don't make me do this again, please?"

Miles' grin promised nothing and I heaved a sigh of exasperation before I walked out of the church and into the blinding November sun. As soon as I was down the steps, Mrs. Morgan accosted me.

"Young lady!"

I bit back a tart reply. "Yes, Mrs. Morgan?"

"I thought I had warned you not to go running after Pastor Jenkins."

"Yes, ma'am," I replied. "You did. I chose to follow God's words rather than yours." A barely stifled laugh behind me warned me that my fiancé was listening in.

"And you, Pastor Jenkins!" Mrs. Morgan turned her attention on him. "How could you even dare to think of marrying someone who is still practically a heathen?"

"Mrs. Morgan," Miles drawled, "iffen Anna is a heathen, that must mean that most of the people in the congregation are also heathens, or worse, since Anna is one of only a very few of my congregants to ever ask me questions about the

228

Bible, Christian living, or something to do with what I preached about the previous Sunday." He raised his hand to pause her protest. "I know that some people are able to figure it out by themselves, but I don't know of anyone who has ever been able to figure it all out by themselves. It is no shame to have to ask someone else for a little clarification.

"And even if it wasn't for that, I would still say the same thing. Anna's life dramatically changed for the better and she acts more like a genuine Christian than anyone else I know, myself included."

My eyes went wide at this statement and I turned toward him. I was about to ask him about it when Mrs. Morgan cut in, "Well! I can see she has somehow gotten her talons in deep and has somehow seduced you into believing every word she says."

Miles' face went hard as granite. "Mrs. Morgan, it was I who asked her to consider allowing me to court her. It was I who asked her to consider becoming more than friends. And it was I who asked her to marry me. Anna did not have a single thought about such things until John brought it up."

"Likely story," Mrs. Morgan huffed. "If you really want to throw your entire life, career, and income away for this woman, you go right ahead. But don't expect me to let this matter go lightly." With that she stormed away.

I sat down hard on the step just above my shaky legs and buried my head in my hands.

"What was that all about?" Wilma's voice asked seconds later.

"Mrs. Morgan has declared war," Miles replied in a flat voice. "She doesn't trust my judgment and

229

thinks that Anna dug her talons in me to seduce me."

"That's ridiculous!" Wilma exclaimed. "Let me at her!" I heard the anger in her voice and raised my head to see her jaw clenched and rage seething out of her green eyes.

"Wilma, it won't do any good. If anything, that would make it worse." I took a deep, calming breath and whispered under my breath, "I just hope this doesn't cost Miles his job."

I heard nothing about the rumors and gossip going around town until four days later when I went to the butcher shop to get some meat for the Jenkins' dinner. While I waited for Mr. Jones to cut and wrap the meat, his wife, a large, cheerful Negro woman came up to me with a serious look on her face.

"You heard what's been goin' 'round about you and Pastor Jenkins?" she asked.

My breath caught. "No, I haven't. And from the look on your face, I don't think I want to." I grimaced and she gave a half smile.

"No, you probably don't, but one o' you two should and I'm guessin' Pastor Jenkins won't hear it either."

I nodded, but remained silent.

"They's saying you're expecting already and that's why you are getting married."

I forced a laugh out. "I guess Miles should have told them we weren't getting married until

February. Their story doesn't make sense then. Not that it makes sense any other way, but…"

Hester's hearty laugh filled the small shop. "I like it, Miz Anna. But that's not all they're sayin'."

"I thought that was getting off a bit too easy."

Hester's smile faded as something caught her eye outside. "Miz Morgan's comin' in here. They're also sayin' you're trying to take over the church and they won't have it. They'll kick Pastor Jenkins out before they let that happen."

My mouth fell open and I worked to control my anger as the bell above the door tinkled. I turned my head to see Mrs. Morgan come in with a glare on her face. She looked between Hester and me. I was afraid she would say something derogatory about Hester again, but Mr. Jones spared us from whatever she might have said.

"Be with you in a minute, Mrs. Morgan," Hester's husband said. "Miss Stuart, your meat is ready."

I took a quick step to the counter. "Thank you, Mr. Jones. How much is it?"

Mr. Jones waved his hand. "Consider it a rather early wedding present for the pastor. Did I hear something about a February wedding?" He took a quick glance toward Mrs. Morgan and gave me a subtle wink.

Despite the horror I felt from the rumors, I had to fight a laugh at Mr. Jones' obvious hint. "Thank you. And yes, you did hear something about that. Miles doesn't think we can get a replacement for him for a week before February."

"A week?" Mrs. Morgan said.

I turned to face her. "Yes. We need someone

231

to marry us and we also need someone to take the pulpit that Sunday." I willed my cheeks to not redden. "He wants to take me on a short honeymoon trip."

"But you won't be married until February? How scandalous!" Mrs. Morgan protested.

"Why is it so scandalous?" I asked.

Mrs. Morgan huffed. "Well, because we all know you must be expecting or the Pastor wouldn't think it necessary to marry you. Who is the father, anyway? Is it Pastor Jenkins or someone else?"

I leaned my back against the counter. "There is no father because there is no child," I said through clenched teeth. "Now if you will excuse me, I need to get this meat home and start cooking it for Miles, John, and James' supper tonight."

"You're not staying for supper tonight?" Mrs. Morgan asked in a falsely sweet voice.

"I never stay for supper at their house," I said as I brushed past her.

"Never?" Mrs. Morgan asked.

I stopped at the door. "No, never. They eat supper at our house every Tuesday, but I have to make supper for my brother and da the other nights. Even if I didn't, I still wouldn't stay."

Mrs. Morgan exhaled loudly. "Well! I still don't think it is right."

"What?" I protested. "That the pastor should choose his own wife from whomever he wishes? Or is your problem that he chose me instead of some handpicked person you wanted?"

Mrs. Morgan stood there with her mouth open. "Well!" she huffed. "I will thank you never to speak to me that way again. Good day!" She stuck her nose in the air and pushed me aside in her haste to leave the butcher shop.

"So," Mr. Jones said, "do you suppose she came here for some meat or to hassle Miss Stuart?"

I took a deep breath and gave him a weak smile. "I think probably the latter. Thank you again for the meat and the warning. Hopefully I haven't made things worse."

"I doubt you could do that," Hester replied.

"Thank you again," I said as I opened the door and hurried back to the parsonage.

I was waiting on the porch when Miles got home.

"Uh oh," he teased. "Did the boys misbehave again?"

"No. Mrs. Morgan," I said in a flat voice.

Miles' smile disappeared. "What now?"

"Well, one of the rumors is that I got myself..." I swallowed hard, "with child and you are marrying me to kind of hide it. She even accused you of being the father."

Miles' jaw dropped open. "What? That's not true at all."

"Exactly."

"And that is only one of the rumors?" Miles leaned against the railing at the bottom of the porch steps and ran his hand through his hair.

"Yes. The other is that I am trying to take over the church and they won't allow that to happen. They would rather kick you out before I get my hands on it. Who 'they' are, I don't know."

Miles closed his eyes and took a deep breath before letting it out in a controlled manner. "Lord, give us strength to get through this trial." He sighed. "Why can't a man choose whoever he wants as his wife without people getting so riled about it?" He opened his eyes and looked at me. "I'm sorry."

I started. "Sorry about what?"

A forced laugh came out of Miles' mouth. "I'm sorry you are caught up in all of this and that you may have to move away from your family if they succeed in kicking me out of the church. I didn't think they would do such a thing. Or go so far as to accuse you of...that." He sat down with a thud on one of the steps and rolled his neck around to work out the kinks. "I think I will change my sermon topic for this week. Not that any of them will listen, but maybe a few will." He took a deep breath and turned his gaze to the setting sun. "I'm sorry, I've kept you too long. You should get home or Caleb and Iain'll have a late supper."

"The boys are probably wondering what's taking you so long as well," I said.

As Miles stood up, he looked at me and asked, "How did you find out about this gossip?"

I gave him a half-grin. "Hester told me. She thought one of us should know. And yes, I thanked her for telling me." I had just passed him when I realized something else he needed to know. "Oh, I also had a small run-in with Mrs. Morgan. I told her in no uncertain terms that I am not with child, that we are getting married in February, that you are trying to find someone to fill the pulpit the first Sunday so you can take me on a honeymoon trip, and that I don't eat supper with you at your house."

"Huh? I understand the first three, but that last one?"

Laughter bubbled up inside of me at the face Miles made. "Because she asked if I was staying for supper tonight."

"Oh."

"Speaking of which, I really need to go. I will see you tomorrow."

"Yes," Miles said, gazing into the darkening landscape, "See ya."

CHAPTER NINETEEN

Thanksgiving and Christmas loomed in the very near future with the wedding coming quickly behind them. I did all I could to keep two households running smoothly as well as preparing for all the events coming up, but I couldn't do it. One day, Wilma came over for a visit.

"Anna, darling, you look terrible!" Wilma exclaimed as I opened the door.

I gave an unconvincing laugh. "That's a nice thing for a friend to say."

"Well, it's true. You look exhausted, your hair is a disaster of knots and your dress isn't buttoned straight. What are you trying to do?"

I held the door open and Wilma stepped inside. "Okay, this has to stop right now, Anna," Wilma said. "You have to slow down a little or tell somebody no. Or something." She spun around and took in the horrifying sight that was the Stuart house.

The house was a disaster and I didn't realize it

until I really looked at it for the first time. Material was strewn around the living room, the kitchen hadn't been swept in ages and the breakfast dishes had yet to be washed.

Wilma turned back to me with a glare. "I repeat: what are you trying to do?"

I blinked at her, unseeing. "Making sheets for my hope chest."

"Anna Aishlinn Stuart, do you mean to tell me that you don't even have your hope chest filled with things yet?"

I nodded my head and Wilma's jaw dropped. "How is that possible?"

"Mama died when I was nine. I never had another mother figure to help me and I was always too busy for suitors and then I was too old. I never had, or felt, a need to get it ready." I shrugged. "So now I'm trying to get it ready."

Wilma collapsed into the nearest chair. "Oh, Anna. You should have asked for help."

I sniffed. "From whom? My only friends have families of their own to take care of and plenty to do for themselves."

"I'll organize a quilting bee with Hester helping behind the scenes. And then the two of us will talk to our husbands about taking a day every week to help you with whatever is needed. And I won't take no for an answer, Anna. You need this more than you know you do. I will also talk Miles into giving you have a day off every week to prepare for your wedding."

I took a deep breath and let it out. "Okay."

"And right now, I am going to wash your dishes while you get that material out of the living room in whatever way you want to."

"Are you always this bossy?" I asked.

"Only when my best friend needs me to be," Wilma replied with a wink.

We both laughed and got to work.

Two hours later, the dishes were done, the linen was one step closer to becoming a sheet, and lunch was on the table. Wilma and I had even managed to do some talking.

That night after dinner, Caleb took the boys out to the barn to help with the evening chores so Miles and I could talk.

"Wilma stopped by the church today. She's concerned about you," Miles said.

"I know. She stopped by here and helped out this morning."

"She asked me to give you a day off so you can get ready for the wedding. What worries me is if this causing you so much stress, why didn't you come to me and ask me that yourself?" Miles' penetrating stare bored into me as I washed the plate.

"I thought I could do it," I said in a quiet voice.

"And you didn't want me to think you couldn't?"

I clenched my jaw and closed my eyes. "Something like that."

"I didn't think of it until Wilma pointed it out, but you shouldn't be expected to prepare for a wedding and keep two households running at the same time. That is more than any woman should ever have to do." He picked up another plate and dried it. "How do Thursdays sound for your day off?"

239

"Are you sure you can do that?"

"Yes."

I turned and looked him full in the eye. "Even with the church people breathing down your neck waiting for you to falter somewhere so they can kick you out?"

A smile tugged at the corners of Miles' mouth. He leaned his hip against the corner. "The most important thing I can ever do is to take care of my family. We may not be married yet, but I still consider you part of my family. If that means I need to work from home so my sons don't run wild, I will figure out a way to do that. Your priority right now needs to be your relationship with God, your family, and getting yourself prepared for the wedding. My family should be your lowest priority. The boys can both help Caleb and Iain when they are here, and you are more than welcome to bring your sewing or whatever to the parsonage to work on while you are there."

"Thank you, Miles. I am sorry I didn't come to you earlier, but I didn't realize how bad I was until Wilma showed up. I've always pushed myself. Ever since I was nine, I've had to work harder than I thought I would be able to handle. I've never known how bad I am until someone tells me."

Miles scowled. "Why didn't Caleb notice?"

I turned back to the soapy water and gave a little laugh. "He's seen me like this before and didn't think anything of it. I'm known in my family for working myself to death."

Miles cocked an eyebrow and took the silverware away from me. "Really? Well, we'll have to see what we can do to break you of that habit."

He winked at me as we heard little feet outside. "Oh! I almost forgot. I've been thinking about Thanksgiving and Christmas. Since Iain doesn't particularly like us at the moment, and it will be your last set of holidays with just the three of you, I was thinking that we should each have our own Thanksgiving and Christmas. Next year, maybe you and Caleb's wife can decide which holiday is at which house."

A smile slowly spread across my face. "That is a wonderful idea! Thank you for thinking of that. But, who will make your meals?"

Miles held up his hands. "Whoa there, Miss Stuart." He backed me up and pinned me against the counter. "Before you came to help, I was the main cook in the family," he whispered, his face mere inches from mine. My breathing was shallow and I had the sudden thought that Miles would kiss me right then and there. "I can cook a Thanksgiving and Christmas meal one last time before handing the reins over to you."

Miles stepped away from me without kissing me and a disappointed sigh came from behind Miles. He spun around to see James standing in the doorway.

"I was hoping you two would kiss," James complained.

Miles gave me a sheepish look. "Not until our wedding and even then, you won't be seeing it."

"Why not?" James asked.

"Because we would both like to keep our first kiss special and private," Miles answered.

"How are you going to do that?" questioned James.

241

"I don't know exactly how yet," Miles said. "Where is John?"

"He's still outside, petting the kittens."

"James," Miles said, "please go out and tell John it is time to leave. I'll meet you two by the front door."

James' lips stuck out in a pout, but he complied.

"In some ways I wish we'd decided on a January wedding," Miles said.

"Why?" I asked, cocking my head to the side.

"Because I don't like that you or I always have to leave. If we were married, we could continue talking all the time except when one of us is gone or when we are asleep. And because I really would like to kiss you. But don't tell James that." His devilish grin returned at the pretend glare I gave him.

"So you have no reservations about marrying me?"

"None," he answered.

"Even though we have only known each other for just over a year and I've only been a genuine Christian for the same length of time? Besides the minor facts such as you possibly losing your job and me not really being fit to be a pastor's wife."

Miles took my hands in his. "Yes. We may not have known each other long, but I feel like I know you better than I knew my first wife when we were married. Sure, we knew many things about each other, but we were so comfortable with each other that we never really talked about deep things like you and I do. And you are the most committed Christian I know in this community. Your enthusiasm puts me to shame at times. That's a good thing, by the way. As for losing my job, that is always in God's hands."

He paused and pulled me one step closer. "And about you becoming a pastor's wife. I think you will make the best pastor's wife this town has ever seen. Even if all you do is raise John and James and keep me focused, you will be wonderful. I am absolutely certain of that."

A knock came on the front door. "Pa? You comin'?" John's question was muffled as his voice came through the door. Miles chuckled and let me go.

"I'll see you tomorrow morning," he said.

I waved as he left. My voice refused to work. No matter how many times I asked him the same questions, Miles always had the same answer. Maybe someday it would beat its way into my head and I would truly believe it.

Despite what I said to Mrs. Morgan and Miles' efforts in person and from the pulpit, the war against us continued. James came home from school the Friday after my first day off with a downcast face.

I heard the kitchen door open and wondered why John had gone around back.

"What's the matter, James?" I asked.

"The kids at school were teasing us something awful today, Miss Stuart," James signed.

"What about?" I asked.

"Just some old lies someone's spreading about

you and Pa."

My heart stopped beating and I had trouble catching my breath. "What kind of lies, James?" At the stubborn look coming to his eyes, I knelt down and grabbed his shoulders. "Please tell me, James. I need to know."

James pursed his lips together and closed his eyes. "They said you were pregnant and that's the only reason Pa's marrying you. And they said you were going to force Pa to do things at church." His hands paused and his shoulders trembled. A stray tear found its way through his eyelid. "They said you didn't really like us and you were only pretending to be kind but as soon as your baby was born you would kick us out of the house." James threw his arms around me in a tight hug and sobbed.

"Shh, shh, James. You know I wouldn't do that. Shh."

"That's not all," John said from the doorway.

I pivoted as best I could with James practically in my lap. I looked up at John and saw why he had gone to the kitchen door instead of front door.

"John! What…"

John held up his free hand. The other hand held a wet rag to his face. "When the boys said you were pregnant, I started getting mad. Then they went on to saying how you would force Pa to change the church and kick us out. I was madder'n a wet hen." John removed the rag from his face. "I fought 'em, Miss Stuart. I know I shouldn't't've, but I did it. It was two against one because I refused to let James get involved and sent him in to get the teacher."

I was heartsick and I worked hard to keep my

244

breathing controlled. James had stopped sobbing by now and could stand on his own two feet. I stood up and took the rag from John. "Didn't the teacher stop the fight?"

John nodded. "After I got a black eye, and some other bruises and had gotten a few licks on them." He tried to give me a half smile, but it ended up being a grimace.

"What'd they do, aim for your head only?" I asked as I led him into the kitchen.

"Naw, they landed a few to my gut, but those don't hurt right now."

I sat him on a chair and got some cold water in a bowl. "James, go get me some more rags, please."

When James came back, I cleaned John up as best I could. "Normally, I don't condone fighting, but this time..." I looked away. "This time, I want to thank you for standing up for me and your da."

I stood up and looked at the two boys. "You two stay here and eat your snack. If you can, get some homework done. If you can't, John, just lie down or whatever you need to in order to help you feel better."

"Where are you going?" John asked.

"I'm going to talk to your father," I said. "This war has gone far enough."

"What war?"

I looked back at them. "The war against your father and me getting married."

I turned on my heel and walked out the door before they could ask any more questions. I marched right into the church and to Miles' small office.

At my deliberate knock, Miles' head snapped up. "Anna? What are you doing here?" The look on my face must have finally registered. "Now what's wrong?"

A grin tried to peek out at his resigned tone of voice. "I'm sorry to bother you on a Friday, but I thought this was more important than finalizing your sermon for the week."

Both of Miles' eyebrows went up and he leaned back in his chair, crossing his arms above his head. "Okay. It is obvious you are ready and have aimed, now shoot."

I took a deep breath and told him what had happened at school earlier that day.

Miles kept an impassive face throughout my entire speech. "What is your recommendation, Miss Stuart?"

I collapsed into the chair across from his desk. "We call together the whole town and try to talk some sense into them. But, since that probably isn't possible, pull John and James out of school until this all blows over. I can teach them at home."

"Isn't that taking the coward's way out?" Miles asked.

"No. It is looking out for their safety."

"Excuse me, Pastor Jenkins?" a male voice spoke from the doorway.

"Yes, Mr. Matthews?" Miles asked.

"I was hoping I could speak to you about a little matter that happened at school today," he said with a grin.

"You may wait outside in the sanctuary until I am finished speaking to Miss Stuart," Miles stated.

Mr. Matthews hemmed and hawed a little.

"Do you have a problem with my request?" Miles asked.

"Yes, actually I do. I know this young lady is your fiancée, and she probably has more of an opportunity…"

"Not this time," Miles interrupted. "But before you go, may I ask you one question?"

"Certainly," the schoolteacher responded.

"Good. Why did it take you so long to break up the fight between John and the three other boys?"

"Um, well," Mr. Matthews stammered, "that's actually what I wanted to talk to you about. I didn't know they were fighting until it was almost over and…"

"Which is why my son James went in to get you as it was starting." Miles stood up. "Mr. Matthews, did James come to tell you about the fight or not?"

"Sending a mute boy in to tell the teacher something is a great folly," Mr. Matthews said as he straightened up.

"Which is why we specifically hired you as the schoolteacher. Because you know sign language." Miles took a step closer to the schoolteacher. "Did you, or did you not, know the fight was going on when it first began? And if so, why did it take you so long to get out there? Do you realize my son could have been seriously injured? If I hadn't taught him to defend himself with his fists, he could have been killed out there and you would have let him." Miles was standing nose to nose with the frightened schoolteacher.

I had just risen to try to calm Miles down when Miles backed up a few steps. "I'm sorry, Mr.

Matthews. That was uncalled for."

Mr. Matthews straightened his collar. "No, Pastor Jenkins. You were right. I was negligent. It won't happen again. That is why I wanted to come talk to you. I wanted to tell you what happened and also let you know I have talked to the parents of the other three and the students themselves. The other three students have been suspended and will not be returning to school until next school term." Mr. Matthews turned toward me. "I apologize for the intrusion, Miss Stuart."

"That's quite all right. You helped our discussion. We were trying to decide what to do next. Any ideas on how to stop a rumor from spreading and causing a wildfire?"

Mr. Matthews shook his head. "I wish I did, Miss Stuart. Good day and thank you for your time."

Miles sank into his chair and closed his eyes. "Now what?"

"I don't know. Try letting the rumor burn itself out and pray for the best?"

"That may be the only choice we have," Miles said. "Someday, I hope we can look back at this and laugh about it."

"Me, too, Miles," I said. "Me, too."

December came and was almost gone before I knew it. Every Thursday, Hester and Wilma came over to my house to help me make things for my hope chest. The quilting bee was a failure because of the rumors, so Hester, Wilma, and I made the quilt together as well. As difficult as it was to be rejected by the rest of the town, it was wonderful to have two close friends. During our times together, I learned that Wilma had learned French from a French spinster in her hometown and that Hester could sing like an angel as well as many other fun tidbits.

Caleb was quiet about his letters with Maggie, but from the eagerness in his face when I handed him each letter, I knew he was anxious to meet her. As was I. Any woman who could occupy my brother's thoughts as much as this woman obviously did was a winner in my mind. The added bonus was that she and her daughter Rachel were getting him to think about God.

When Christmas came, Da wanted it to be a quiet day, so we all sat around, stuffed our faces with food and talked about Christmases past.

"Remember the year we hid the presents on Mama and Da?" Caleb asked.

I threw my head back and let loose a laugh. "Do I ever! That was one of the best Christmases ever!"

"Yes, it was," Caleb replied, a flicker of sadness in his eyes. "It was the Christmas we learned we would have a new brother or sister."

"That's right!" I exclaimed. "Mama and Da told us on Christmas Eve. And that's when we plotted to hide the presents. We got up really early and carried them all into the barn. Then we went back to bed and pretended to be very sad when we saw all the presents were gone."

"And then I went out to do chores while Aishlinn made breakfast," Da said. "And I found

249

the presents hiding under a pile of hay."

I chuckled and sighed. "I wish Mama and Jed were here."

"Your Mama's not here because of Jed," Da spat.

"Da!" Caleb warned. "Don't start that up now. Not on Christmas Day."

I ignored Da's comment and closed my eyes. "I remember our last Christmas with Jed. He was so excited because he had figured out the best present to give to each of us. He cooked breakfast for me and did all of the morning chores for Caleb and Da. Then under the tree, he wrapped up slips of paper and told us what he had done for us that morning and that he would do it for the rest of the year."

Caleb's hearty laugh reached to the rafters. "I remember that. Da was shocked. So was I."

"I was shocked he knew how to crack an egg, let alone cook one," I said.

"Next year..."

"Next year there willna be a Christmas like any in the past," Da ranted. "Me two children'll be married and have their own Christmases with their wee bairns."

"Nay, Da," I protested. "We'll all have Christmas together with you and both of our families. It'll be grand fun. Just you wait and see, Da."

"Aye," Caleb said with a wink at me. "And maybe my sister will have a little girl of her own by then."

"Caleb Iain Stuart! I am much too old to be thinking about things like that. And a little girl?

You cannot be serious!"

"You are only thirty, Anna. Mama had Jed when she was almost forty and there are many other women who have children into their forties. And yes, you need a little girl to pamper like you always wished you had been."

I huffed and stood up. "I need to get the kitchen cleaned up and you have chores to do, Caleb." The last word had a bit of a bite to it. But secretly, my heart warmed to the idea of having a baby girl of my own to hold and cherish by this time next year. *But, God, I've never taken care of a girl. I wouldn't know how to raise a girl.*

Trust God, Anna! I scolded myself.

Yes, Ma'am, I answered as I attacked the dishes.

After the New Year, Miles was able to find a fill-in preacher for him on the second Sunday of February. Which meant we would be married on Saturday, February 8, 1879. I hadn't been nervous about the wedding before, but when the date was set and the preacher was booked, then I started to get very nervous. For over a month, I hadn't had any doubts about marrying Miles, but they suddenly came flooding back to me and Miles had to give me quite a few talks about it.

January sped by with lots of cold weather and some rain. Wilma, Hester, and I got everything finished by the end of January and began working on my dress. Yes, we only had a week, but with three of us sewing, we had it done in plenty of time.

Oh, God, can it be true? I found myself asking this question every day from the first of the year on into February. The Friday before the wedding, I was a nervous wreck and was eternally grateful Miles decided to keep the boys at home all that week without me coming over or them coming here. I would never have survived them.

That night, I tossed and turned as my rattled nerves brought visions of doubts and answers coming into my mind. I finally prayed and God gave me the peace I needed to get a few hours of sleep before the biggest day of my life. The day I would become Miles Jenkins' wife.

CHAPTER TWENTY

Mama, I wish you could be here to see me, my mind wept as I waited for Da. *Would you be proud of me or disappointed like Da? I know Da is disappointed I am marrying a Pastor, but what about you, Mama? Oh, I think you would be proud of me, but what if you would have changed like Da did?* I shook my head.

Anna, you are being ridiculous! Of course Mama would be proud of you. I took a deep breath and tried to smile when I saw Wilma heading toward me.

"You look lovely, Anna!" Wilma exclaimed. "Oh my lands, but I do believe you are the most beautiful bride I've ever seen."

My cheeks burned. "I am not and you know it, Mrs. Gardner!"

"Au contraire, Mademoiselle Stuart, you truly are the most beautiful bride I have seen. Don't you agree, Darius?"

I looked past Wilma to her husband.

"The second most beautiful, Wilma. You were the most beautiful. No offense to you, Miss Stuart," Darius smiled at me.

I fought a grin and said, "I would have taken offense for Wilma's sake, if you would have said anything other than that."

Darius smiled and nodded at me. "I'd better head in and calm Miles down. He was acting rather nervous when I last saw him."

Wilma scowled at Darius and waved him away. "Finally," she exclaimed, "We are alone! How are you doing?"

"I'm nervous," I said, taking a deep breath. I spoke quickly as I always did when nervous. "Am I really doing the right thing? We've known each other for just over a year. Yes, I love the boys, but do I love Miles? Is what I am feeling truly love? It's all so confusing! And then there's the fact that Miles could lose his job because of me. Is that a sign we aren't supposed to marry each other? Can I really be a pastor's wife? I grew up without really knowing God and I know very little. And I have been a Christian for just over a year. Am I really the right choice for Miles?"

Wilma put her hands up on my shoulders. "Anna. You and Miles have talked about this endless times. I know you have because you keep on telling me about it. Your fears are justified, but since you have been over it a million times between the two of you and also with God, I truly believe your becoming the wife of Miles, the mother of John and James, and the wife of the pastor is God's perfect plan for this church. The church needs it, the town needs it, and more than that, Miles and the boys need it."

I closed my eyes and drew in a deep breath. "Are you sure?" My voice was barely above a whisper.

"I am absolutely sure," she said. She looked behind me. "And it looks like they are ready for us, Anna. Let's go do this! Let's go make you Miles Jenkins' wife."

The butterflies in my stomach fluttered with the speed of lightning. Back and forth. Back and forth. I tried to grab at Wilma's hand, but she evaded me. And then suddenly, I was standing in front of my da.

Da stared at me and looked me up and down. His Adam's apple bobbed up and down a few times as he swallowed. "Anna," he whispered, "you look so much like yer mither." He closed his eyes and took a deep breath. "Let's get you down that aisle to the man waiting for ye."

I held out my right arm and he hooked his elbow into mine. I put my left hand on top of his arm and gave him a little squeeze. "Thank ye, Da."

Da nodded at me and walked me toward the door leading to the church. As we climbed the steps I prayed silently, "Lord, are you sure I am doing the right thing here? I need Your guidance." An overwhelming peace spread throughout my body as John and James opened the double doors for Da and me to walk through. I smiled at them as we passed by and I looked up at Da with a joyful smile. Together, we stepped through the church doors and Da gave me away to the man who far exceeded any I could have dreamed for. God knew my vision before I did and made it more than I had ever thought possible.

Keep reading for a special preview of

AMAZING GRACE

Hymns of the West #3
by Faith Blum

Coming in early 2015!

Caleb hurried to the post office. He had to get in and out before his sister finished at the general store. "Any mail for the Stuarts?" He asked the post master.

The post master took a lazy look at him over the top of his eyeglasses and gave a heaving sigh as he turned around to check. "Yep. Somethin' from Ohio and somethin' from Montana."

Caleb waited until the large man put the letters lazily in his hand. As he left he wondered why Anna had written someone in Montana. It was really none of his business, but he was still curious. He folded the Ohio letter and stashed it in his back pocket. It would get wrinkled, but at least Anna wouldn't know about it.

As he waited, he tapped his toes as the time crept along. Why did women always take so long to shop? He thought about pulling the letter out and starting to read it, but he knew that as soon as he did, Anna would come out and catch him reading it.

"Sorry I took so long, Caleb," Anna looked at her brother with chagrin as she came out of the store fifteen minutes later than she had said she would. "I got caught up talking to Wilma and Hester."

Caleb shrugged. "'S'okay." He helped Anna climb up onto the wagon seat and waited for her to scoot over before he climbed up beside her. As he gathered the reins, he remembered Anna's letter.

"Oh, there was a letter for you. It's from Montana."He looked at her with a question on his face as he held the letter toward her.

Anna snatched it from him with a grin. "That was fast. I just wrote them a few weeks ago."

"Who'd ya write to?"

"Joshua Brookings and his family."

"The sheriff that hanged Jed?"

Anna sighed. "Sheriff Brookings didn't hang Jed, he led Jed to Christ. Well, with help."

Caleb nodded. "What'd you write them about?"

"I wanted to thank them for helping my little brother out."

Caleb couldn't think of anything to say after that, especially when Anna started to sniffle. She wasn't usually emotional, but she'd been through a lot in the last twenty years of her life and Jed's death had added to it. Caleb sighed inwardly. They'd all been through a lot the last twenty years.

Especially during the war years. As the horses trotted past the church, a similar, but vastly different scene flashed into his mind.

* * *

He had led the troops to a church where they claimed the enemy had encamped. Without even scouting to see if anyone was there, the general ordered the artillery to open fire.

Caleb had never been much of a church-loving person, but he had some respect for the buildings and those who worshiped there. He clamped his mouth shut, knowing that one word of dissension from him could get him killed and then where would Da, Anna, and Jed be?

* * *

Caleb blinked rapidly as the fields came into view. He glanced over at Anna to make sure she hadn't noticed anything. She hadn't. She was engrossed in her letter. He sighed quietly in relief before pulling back on the reins and setting the brake as the wagon came to a halt between the house and the barn.

"I'll get the packages," Anna said, looking up from the letters. "You should take care of the horses and get back out to help Da."

Caleb gave a mock salute. "Yes, Ma'am."

Anna rolled her eyes. "Sorry, I guess I was bein' a little bossy there."

"That's all right," Caleb drawled. "I kin take it once in awhile. Just not too often, y'hear?" He wagged his finger at her and she chuckled.

"Yes, Sir, I'll try not to."

As Anna cooked supper, she thought about the encouraging letter she had received from the Brookings family. On a whim, she had written to them a few months after she became a Christian. Now she was glad that she had. Harriet Brookings had decided to take it upon herself to mentor Anna in her new role as surrogate mother to the pastor's sons. Now that she was being courted by Miles, Anna hoped to get some more advice from her.

Her smile dipped a little as she thought about her da. "God," she prayed, "Please show Da Your love. He desperately needs you." She cut her prayer short when she heard boots on the porch outside. Maybe Caleb would go to bed early tonight and she could reply to Harriet's letter. Anna scurried around the kitchen, a smile lighting up her face as she finished putting supper on the table.

As soon as the evening chores were finished, Caleb rushed upstairs, lit the candle beside his bed and grabbed the letter out of his pocket. He ripped the envelope open and pulled the letter out. A sudden feeling of panic hit him all of a sudden and he closed his eyes and took a deep, steady breath.

When his lungs couldn't hold any more air, Caleb let it out slowly. As the last of the breath escaped his lungs, Caleb opened his eyes a crack, then a crack more, until they were fully open and staring at the beautiful handwriting of Maggie McDougall.

Dear Mr. Stuart,
I appreciate your honesty. If there is one thing lacking in men these days—at least here in Wheeling—it is honesty. It seems that men will do

anything to get what they want. Enough of that though. I don't think you really want me to analyze all the men here and write it down on paper for you.

As I said in the ad, I am 30 years old so your sister and I must be about the same age. I grew up on a farm and, though I loved my husband enough to move to the city, I have always wanted to be out in the country again, especially as Rachel gets older. She is already becoming a beautiful young woman and I fear for her safety in this city.

About myself, I have thick brown hair, brown eyes, and am well tanned from my days growing up on the farm. I think I have lost some of the tan while living in the city.

I am truly sorry to hear about your brother's death. Did you get to see him before he died? If I may, why has your sister been so different since hearing about Jed's death?

I'm not sure what to say about myself either as I am also new to this. One thing I should tell you is that I am replying to two letters I have received so far and will be asking both of you tough questions to try to figure out which situation and man God wants me to marry.

I do understand. I also want to get married, but don't. I honestly don't know if I could ever love another man the way I loved Duncan and that seems unfair to the man I might marry in the future.

I know you aren't a Christian (yet) but I would like to say that God already knows what is in your past and He still wants you to be His child. I challenge you to read the Bible, especially Genesis, John, and Acts. Those books tell about faithful men of God who screwed up and God still forgave them. They also are good books for learning more about what Christianity is all about. What kinds of things are you having a hard time dealing with?

I placed the ad because both Rachel and I had the idea the same day and we both felt like God was telling me to do it. I have also had an almost impossible time finding steady work. I can find an odd job here and there, but unless I become a lady of the street, I can't find anything permanent. As you have probably figured out, my daughter's name is Rachel and she absolutely loves the idea of getting a new father.

I have been widowed for two years. Duncan was at his job doing construction on a house and fell from the roof, breaking his back. He died a few days later. It is hard to talk about, but I need to talk about it, so I don't mind answering.

How are things on the farm? What is your sister like? Is she married? When you aren't working on the farm, what do you like to do? Do you take Sundays off? If so, what do you do? I wish I didn't have to ask this, but I do. Do you drink alcoholic beverages? Why did you reply to my ad?

Sincerely,
Maggie McDougall

As he read the last word, he let the letter fall to the floor. She'd actually written him back and she'd him written a long letter. And she was a lady in distress! Not that it really mattered, but ever since his mother had read those fairy tales out loud at bedtime, he had dreamed of being a prince in shining armor. Or was it a knight in shining armor? He shrugged. Either way, if he somehow managed to win this woman's heart, he might just be able to be that...person in shining armor after all. Only without the armor. And without being a prince or a knight.

He blew out the candle, picked up the letter, put it on his desk and got ready for bed. He lay in bed, staring into the darkness for over an hour according to the grandfather clock downstairs. When the clock chimed ten, Caleb shook his head and hissed to himself, "You are as daft as a schoolboy with his first crush. This is ridiculous! Get over it already!" With that, he rolled over, covered his head with his pillow and went to sleep.

Anna was at church again and Caleb sat at the desk in the parlor muttering to himself about something. Iain scowled. Why didn't his kids just get themselves married? Then he could find peace and quiet without hiding out in the barn. And he could do whatever he wanted without the judgmental looks from Anna and Caleb.

Iain clomped to the barn, refusing to look around as he passed the spot where Jed had beaten him up. He rubbed his side absentmindedly as he walked into the barn. Just before a rain, his ribs would ache where they'd been broken nine years earlier. Iain scowled and darted a glance around the barn as if to make sure no one was hiding inside the dark building.

Once he was assured no one was watching, he strode to his hiding place in the far stall. In the stall, he scooted along the wall and back behind the haystack. He sat down heavily on the floor and reached his hand toward the hidden compartment he had built into the barn floor...how many years ago? Twenty? Twenty-one? He shook his head. "Not today, Iain! Don't think on that today!"

He pulled the bottle out of the compartment and uncorked it. "Just a few gulps o' th' good stuff," he told himself as he tipped the bottle back. "Just enough to take the edge off this pain inside, but not enough to get Anna and Caleb suspicious."

The fiery liquid slid down his throat and into his belly, warming and numbing every inch of his body, including his brain. He rested his head against the barn wall, bent one leg and rested the other leg on his knee. The jug sat clutched in his hands.

As his body grew more and more numb, his mind became more active. Although this wasn't usually the case, it did happen occasionally. His mind went back to the time when he had first started to make his own moonshine.

He'd known if he spent money on liquor Aishlinn would notice and he couldn't have that happen because he couldn't have her know he was drinking again after he'd promised not to. So he built a still and made and drank his own brew. It wasn't too bad, actually. He could even get it pretty good more often than naught.

His stomach clenched and the jug dropped to the barn floor as his thoughts wandered back a little further.

Aishlinn had just miscarried a second time in as many years since Anna's birth.

"If she gets pregnant again," the doctor said to him, "your wife might not survive. Don't have any more children. She won't survive the birthing for sure and maybe not even the pregnancy."

Iain had been in shock and couldn't say a word. In the present, a rogue tear worked its way down his wrinkled cheek. He'd turned to drink for his solace as often as he dared. Except for that one time when he'd turned to his wife. What had that God of Aishlinn's been thinking to let her get pregnant? Why couldn't...

Iain clenched his jaw and punched the stall wall, scraping his knuckles and causing Storm to shuffle and whinny in the stall next to him.

He looked up. The sun had stopped streaming through the barn door when Iain looked up from the floor. Anna would be getting back soon. That daft girl had started going to church again and didn't care that he'd forbidden her from going there over ten years before. Iain grunted in disgust. Maybe she'd find some young man there to get hitched to soon.

Iain groaned as he pulled himself up. As he steadied himself against the stall, Storm nuzzled his arm looking for a sugar cube or carrot stick. "Nothin' today, Storm lad. Nothin' today."

He walked into the sun and blinked his eyes. He saw Anna walking up the road and hurried to the house. He ignored the stare his son gave him and went straight to his room. He would avoid Anna until it was time to eat.

SPECIAL THANKS

I would be remiss if I did not say thanks to all the many people who helped me with the publication of this book. Even after doing it all once before, I am still learning and figuring out the whole publication process.

Thank You, God, for being my vision, wisdom, and Savior. You are the only reason I exist in this world for such a time as this.

Thank you to all my beta-readers: Mom, Naomi, Garry, Joanna, Molly, Travis, Andrew, and Valerie. All of your comments—whether spelling, grammar, history, theology, or storyline—were extremely helpful.

Many thanks to Perry for, yet again, doing an awesome job with the book cover and for working with me to find the perfect image. The cover is gorgeous! She also did a wonderful job with the formatting.

Extra special thanks go to Naomi who helped me learn and describe many of the signs for James so I could describe them. Also, thank you Mom, Lydia, and Naomi for spending hours proofreading (including reading parts out loud to Seth) for me! You gals did an awesome job!

If he reads this part of the book, he will probably be surprised to see his name here, but I would like to thank Pastor George. Thank you for being a courageous pastor who stands up for what is right no matter what. While Miles Jenkins isn't really modeled after you, your willingness to talk about the tough issues reminds me of Miles and was an inspiration for him. Thank you!

ABOUT THE AUTHOR

An avid reader, Faith Blum started writing at an early age. Whether it was a story about the camping trip that summer or a more creative story about fictional characters, she has always enjoyed writing. When not writing, Miss Blum enjoys reading, crafting, playing piano, being a Captain on the Holy Worlds Historical Fiction Forum and playing games with her family (canasta, anyone?).

An ardent history enthusiast who has been fascinated for years with the Old West, Faith has endeavored to create a clean, fun, and challenging Western story. Faith lives with her family on a hobby farm in the Northern Midwest, where she enjoys playing with the many cats they have.

To learn more about Faith's other writing projects, and to discover some of the behind-the-scenes development, visit her blog site: http://faithblum.wordpress.com or go to her website: http://www.FaithBlum.com.

Made in the USA
Charleston, SC
04 November 2014